WOUNDED LITTLE GODS

Published by Tuttle Publishing, an imprint of Periplus Editions (HK) Ltd.

www.tuttlepublishing.com

Copyright © Eliza Victoria
www.elizavictoria.com
First published in the Philippines in 2016 by Visprint, Inc.

Cover design and illustrations by Jap Mikel; www.japmikel.tumblr.com
Author photo by Vlad Gonzales

ISBN 978-0-8048-5522-8

Library of Congress Cataloging-in-Publication Data in process

The moral rights of the author and illustrator have been asserted.

Distributed by

North America, Latin America & Europe
Tuttle Publishing
364 Innovation Drive
North Clarendon, VT 05759-9436
U.S.A.
Tel: 1 (802) 773-8930
Fax: 1 (802) 773-6993
info@tuttlepublishing.com
www.tuttlepublishing.com

Japan
Tuttle Publishing
Yaekari Building, 3rd Floor
5-4-12 Osaki
Shinagawa-ku
Tokyo 141 0032
Tel: (81) 3 5437-0171
Fax: (81) 3 5437-0755
sales@tuttle.co.jp
www.tuttle.co.jp

Asia Pacific
Berkeley Books Pte. Ltd.
3 Kallang Sector, #04-01
Singapore 349278
Tel: (65) 67412178
Fax: (65) 67412179
inquiries@periplus.com.sg
www.tuttlepublishing.com

25 24 23 22   7 6 5 4 3 2 1

Printed in Malaysia   2201VP

TUTTLE PUBLISHING® is a registered trademark of Tuttle Publishing, a division of Periplus Editions (HK) Ltd.

WOUNDED LITTLE GODS

a novel

by
Eliza Victoria

TUTTLE Publishing

Tokyo | Rutland, Vermont | Singapore

WOUNDED
LITTLE GODS

PART I

X

CHAPTER 1

Spirits used to roam the town of Heridos.

Regina knew this of course, being born and raised here. But right now, lying in the dark on the side of the road, she felt as if she had to keep telling this story, or else, she would forget who she was.

So.

From the top.

Spirits used to roam the town of Heridos, and then suddenly, they didn't.

As a child, Regina was used to seeing adults making animal sacrifices and offerings to bless a new house, to ask for the end of an illness, or to pray for a bountiful harvest. Regina's grandmother used to say, *Your mother spilled blood to give birth to you, and so too we shall spill blood as an offering to the spirits to give birth to a wish or a dream.* Which sounded beautiful to Regina, but not, as she was fond of saying, something that would sway her vegetarian friends.

(Her parents didn't approve of her jokes, which they found insensitive. Other things they didn't approve of: her whiny complaints about every little inconvenience, like the power going out, the heat, the heavy rain, the long commute, hard pil-

8

lows; her impatience with the slow pace of rural life; her flippant "Work smart, not hard!"; her hatred of backbreaking work that her parents—and her parents' parents, and her parents' parents' parents, and soon since the very beginning of time—took so much pride in.)

Ten years ago, Heridos suffered a poor harvest, which got increasingly poorer as the years went by. It was as though the soil was cursed. The animal sacrifices stopped, and the goats and the pigs and the chickens moved—alive, at least initially—from the fields to the local parish, to the delight of the town priest, who for so long thought his parishioners were being annoying and pagan. Spirits sightings became increasingly rare until no one believed in them anymore. Regina's mother continued to set food aside for the spirits whenever the family had a huge gathering at the house—a birthday, or the Day of the Dead—and her father still asked permission and gave due warning before watering the plants, *Tabi, tabi po*, but they did this more out of habit now than actual belief.

Most of the farmers became store owners, selling vegetables, root crops, and rice sourced from nearby towns. Some became hog and poultry farmers, raising pigs and chickens in backyard kennels and selling them as butchered meat in the wet market. They sold their farmlands to residential and commercial developers, and one of the rice fields gave birth to a mall.

(Though no blood was spilled.)

(At least as far as Regina knew.)

Some of the men and women went abroad and worked in factories in Taiwan or China or the United Arab Emirates, joining the deluge of skilled workers leaving the country to earn more cash for their families. The price of land in town appreciated significantly, and consumer goods, especially food, became much more expensive. The average Heridos house, especially in the Poblacion, transformed from a simple one-story wooden house to a concrete structure with a second-floor terrace and a grotto—the house built by remittance.

What kind of spirits used to live in this town?

Well, imaginary talk show host, these were: the spirits of *palay*, of *alimuom*, of sun, silence, and rain, of clouds and lingering dreams, of the turning earth.

Of the artisanal soda. Of the matte lipstick. Of the hipster meme. Of—well, Regina, you are losing the plot. Now you are just being condescending.

"Are they gods?" Regina once asked her grandmother months before she died of old age. Her grandmother said they were nature personified; entities we could commune with and understand until we were worthy enough—or strong enough—to grasp the complexity and magnitude of *Bathala*.

"So," little Regina said, "they're like secretaries?"

Ten years ago, Ka Edgar, the oldest man in town at the time, said he woke up in the middle of the night and saw a young man (though to an octogenarian, penicillin could be considered young, so Regina took this description with a grain of salt) sitting on the edge of his bed. The young man was trying to tell him something, Ka Edgar said, but he could not understand a word. They weren't even words in the first place, just sounds: a gurgling drainpipe, wind whispering through fields of *palay*, the sound of a person choking on his own blood.

The old man knew it was a spirit trying to give him a message, but he was scared shitless, and what was he to do? The spirit didn't come with an interpreter.

That was the first year of the poor harvest. A sizeable portion of the old man's land produced rice grains as black as soot.

Okay, so that probably wasn't the best thing to think about, Regina, out here in the middle of the night, on this dark road.

Regina was lying on her back, her muscles sore, the back of her head hurting like hell. La Reina Heridos. La Regina Heridos. The wounded queen. The wounded Regina.

She was still trying to sit up. For miles around, all she could see was black against black, an outline of trees and wild grass against the night sky. She couldn't tell how long she had been lying there on the side of the road. She had seen no car or vehicle, or house, or another person. All she could hear was the low, continuous hum of cicadas, like an angry buzzing before an explosion.

So, think, Regina. Think of something else.

Regina thought of—

- attending grade school with OFW swag: the bright-green wristwatch that plays Beethoven's "Für Elise" when you lift the cover; the pencil case with the tiny piano that you can actually play; the ruler filled with water, tinfoil fish, and glitter; the large padded bags filled with markers in 140 colors, from Bittersweet Cerise to Wishful Wisteria
- her father's Taiwanese bosses dropping by for a visit, and her father introducing her and her older brother Luciano in Hokkien because her father knows the Hokkien words for "eldest" and "youngest" and he wants to impress them
- waking up at 3 AM to prepare for the school parade; the beautician sticking curlers in her hair and pumping the

11

atmosphere with hair spray so she'll "look like a little queen", to which she replies with a frown and a deep sigh because it's too early in the morning for this nonsense

- listening to her brother talk about his grade school years, about a classmate who hit his head and bled profusely—"I have never seen that much blood in my life"—and how the classmate got sutures and went on to live in California with his wife—"I think he's into cars now"—and Regina, filled to the brim with coffee, telling her brother how amazing it is that a tragedy today can be forgotten years from now—"Does anyone even mourn Carthage?"
- at the same time thinking of the thirteen-year-old girl who died here on this field, the one who they said ran the length of an entire barangay like a dog pursued before slipping and dying here, in the mud, her father cradling her body in his arms, terror-struck, the look in his eyes promising that he would be haunted by this moment for years and years and years

Oh awesome, Regina. What enlightening material. I feel so comforted now.

Shut up.

Shut up and get up.

A light appeared in the distance. Faint but visible through the trees.

Get up, she told herself. Get up, get up, *get up.*

Regina rolled onto her stomach, took a deep breath, and pushed herself up. (Idly she noted she was doing the beginning of an Elbow Push-Up and a Mountain Climber, two of the moves they taught in that gym class she attended once and then dropped as if it were radioactive.) The whole maneuver took her close to ten minutes.

She walked as if she were drunk, swaying, losing balance. She kept her eyes on the prize, that light in the distance. She was getting closer.

Regina veered right, getting off the road and stepping into a clearing.

The light was coming from a house.

The light was coming from a house that was not supposed to be there.

Wait.

What?

Oh, Regina.

Surely, you're still on the side of the road, enjoying a final hallucination before your untimely demise.

But it didn't feel like a dream. It felt real. (And wouldn't it be too sad if her last dream of this life involved suffering from what appears to be the hangover of the century? That would be too sad.) Regina walked-swayed to the house and placed her hand on the door. Her hand didn't sink through. She knocked, and Florina opened it.

"Regina," Florina said as Regina stared with her mouth open. "There you are."

"What?" Regina said.

CHAPTER 2

A week earlier, Regina was just ending her shift at the small offshore company where she worked as Administrative Assistant. The company took on a lot of jobs from clients in the US, and accepted anyone who could string three words together. Seriously. Anyone. HR was like a revolving door. They prided themselves on their one-day processing, which involved something called "not digging into an applicant's background." This would have a bearing later on in Regina's story.

Regina took the job out of panic. She was fresh out of college with a Journalism degree she had a love/hate relationship with, three of her job applications had already fallen through, and she had bills to pay. The job that was finally offered to her was dumb and repetitive, but the office was in Makati and the pay and the hours weren't bad. Her parents were disappointed in her career choice, and they had made their disappointment known subtly, sometimes overtly. Regina didn't mind. She figured it was still early enough to make mistakes. On the other hand, her brother, who worked as a researcher in Los Baños and earned enough to afford a secondhand car, was simply happy that someone in the city chose to hire her. He set his bar pretty low.

She had been working for close to a month when the company welcomed a graphic designer named Diana. She looked to be in her mid-20s, definitely not entry-level, which made Regina wonder why she would choose to work in a small, borderline-black-market company such as this. They sat in adjoining cubicles next to the huge windows that gave them a view of Ayala Avenue, greeted each other every morning, and said goodbye at 6 PM every night. Diana wasn't very talkative, and Regina would be hesitant to call her a friend. They weren't even Facebook friends.

On Diana's second week at work, the following Monday was proclaimed a holiday, so on Friday she and Diana stood by the windows, nose to the glass, looking on in horror as traffic built up on the streets.

"Shit," Regina said. "Those cars aren't moving."

"This is a nightmare," Diana said. "Where do you live?"

This was Diana's first question to Regina that didn't involve her choice for lunch or *merienda*.

"QC," Regina replied.

"Yikes."

"I know. I'd be stuck on the road if I took a bus, and the train's going to be filled with people." Regina sat down. "I figure I'll just stay here until late at night."

"I live nearby," Diana said. "Want to crash there for a few hours?"

Diana was already packing up her stuff. There were still a handful of people in the office who, like Regina, planned to wait out the weekend gridlock.

"Are you sure?" Regina asked. "It won't be a bother?"

"No, of course not," she said. "It's a studio apartment, but there's space for you to sleep if you want to. We can walk there."

So, they walked. Regina insisted on buying take-out for their dinner. Diana's studio apartment was on the 10th floor of a high-rise building. Her place was cluttered with books and shoes but had a clean, minty smell, like a spa. Diana had an impressive PC setup, the computer sitting on a faux oak table near the door. She appeared to have spent most of her money on the machine, scrimping on the rest of the furniture pieces. She had a coffee table for a dining table, with pillows on the floor as seats. Boxes for bookshelves. A mattress on the floor for a bed.

Regina, who was a bedspacer in a lady's dorm in Quezon City, loved everything.

Diana turned on the PC and played some music as Regina fixed their plates and their food. She glanced at the books stacked under the table. One had a photo of a portion of an art installation from the 1920's. *Some people are born to be a burden on the rest,* the copy read in flowing script.

The books had titles like *The Secret History of Human Experimentation. Holocaust Experiments. Bad Blood. Eugenics: Creating the Master Race.*

"Let's eat," Diana said with a smile. She sat cross-legged across from her and reached for the rice. "Is there anyone you need to call back home?"

"Just my brother I guess," Regina said. "But I've already texted him."

"Older?"

"Yes."

"Are you guys close?"

Regina shrugged. "I guess? But we don't see each other that often."

"Where do you live?" Diana said. "If you don't mind me asking."

"Heridos," Regina said.

"Small town?"

"I wouldn't call it small," she replied, and paused to think. "We now have a Mini-Stop."

Diana laughed. They ate, and talked about work, the people at work ("I never liked that pompous jerk"), and the work they had to return to on Monday even if the rest of the workforce were on holiday because, apparently, they belonged to the continental United States. The whole time Regina kept glancing under the coffee table.

"So," she said, when she couldn't help it any longer, "about your books—"

It seemed as if Diana was just waiting for her to speak. "Some light reading, huh."

"They look—"

Grim? Sad? Strange?

"—interesting."

"I've been reading up on eugenics and human experimentation for a long time," Diana said. "I'm—I can't say I'm *fascinated*. It's not a fascination, really. More like a disbelief. I can't believe it all really happened, and now I can't stop reading. It's like I'm hoping to come across a piece of information that would tell me otherwise."

Regina didn't know how to respond to that.

"For example, the Tuskegee experiment in Alabama. That one ran until 1972, and could have continued running if not for a media leak. It included 400 African-American men with syphilis, who thought they were receiving treatment when, in fact, they were just being used to observe the natural progression of the disease. They were not given treatment even after the discovery of penicillin in 1947. So, of course, these men infected their wives and passed on syphilis to their children.

"Even earlier," Diana said, "something that happened right here. In 1906, an American director of the Philippine Biological Laboratory infected Bilibid inmates with cholera. He did this without the inmates' consent. Thirteen died in that experiment. That doctor became a medical professor at Harvard University.

"And, of course, you've read of what happened during the Third Reich. The Nazis sewed twins together, injected dye into children's eyes, and exposed people to the cold until they died. Prisoners were poisoned or bombarded with mustard gas or infected with tuberculosis, and then killed immediately so doctors could carry out autopsies. Can you believe that? They sound too brutal to be real, and yet they *are* real, they *did* happen.

"The sadder thing is, all these horrible things? *They have happened before.* There were genocides before the Holocaust, and these genocides have already been forgotten. Does anyone even mourn Carthage? You would think—you would hope—that one genocide is one too many, that we would finally learn that every life is precious. That we would try to be better. And yet—"

She stopped suddenly.

"I'm so sorry," Diana said.

"Want some beer?" Regina said at the same time. Diana smiled.

"What a stupid topic to bring up," Diana said.

"It's all right."

"Do you know that I even began writing these ideas into this game I'm working on?"

"A game?"

"Yes. Do you play?" Diana stood up, not waiting for her reply. "Let me show you something."

She talked as she opened windows on her PC. "I have some notes and I've started working on an interactive environment. Just something to play with. Try this. It's more virtual tour right now than game, actually."

Regina sat in the computer chair softened with about ten throw pillows, and moved the mouse. Onscreen were four buildings that, due to the crude CG, looked more like steel boxes with holes. The grass like shards of green glass. Three flies were painted on one wall of the nearest building. Two of the insects, separated by a plus sign, had red eyes; the one beneath, preceded by an arrow, had white eyes. Regina recognized this. For some reason, she wanted to impress Diana. The flies were fruit flies, and they referred to Thomas Hunt Morgan's experiments with—what was the scientific name for fruit fly? Droso-something—Anyway—fruit flies, which proved that genetic changes could happen outside of inheritance, and which he used to criticize eugenics.

Is there a prize for people who solved Easter eggs? Regina wanted to say, feeling clever, but then Diana moved the mouse again and swiped the screen to the right.

More sharp blades of grass, now dotted with gold. *Palay.* Rice ready for harvest.

In the far distance, an outline of a house with what seemed to be a broken roof. Regina stared at this in disbelief. She knew this house, and would recognize this house and that telltale bend of its roof in a heartbeat. As a child she passed by it nearly every day with her parents. It was where Ka Edgar lived. It was abandoned after the old man died, and the roof caved in after a storm.

So instead of the Easter egg quip, all Regina could think to say was *Are you from Heridos, and do we know each other?* as she turned to Diana to demand an explanation.

Diana, sitting on an ottoman she had pulled from one corner of the apartment, stared at the computer screen with tears flowing from her eyes. Regina was shocked and disturbed by this.

"Are you okay?" she asked.

Diana's reflexes were slow. She turned her head, stared at Regina for a few unnerving seconds, and said, "Hm?"

"You know what," Regina said, thinking, *I'm too tired to get involved in this,* "I think the streets are manageable now. I should get out of your hair."

Diana blinked and wiped her face with an open palm. "Are you sure?"

"Yes. I could take the train." Lie. It was already 11 PM, and the MRT was already closed.

"Let me get your bag."

It took Diana a while to retrieve Regina's bag from the floor. She wondered if Diana was on medication and if it was okay to leave her alone.

"Will you be all right?" Regina asked as Diana handed her bag to her.

Diana looked surprised by this. *What? Me? Why wouldn't I be?* "Of course." As though she had not been crying just five minutes ago. "Take care of yourself, okay?"

"See you on Monday?" Regina said.

"Sure."

Lie. Regina did not see Diana on Monday. Or the next day. Or the day after that. The office assumed Diana hated the job too much to even tender a proper resignation and just decided to go AWOL (which in the office was a frequent enough occurrence). Regina was worried. On Wednesday, she told HR about Diana's inexplicable crying on Friday night (omitting the part where Diana started talking at length about Nazi experiments and genocide), and accompanied her supervisors to Diana's building. They met Diana's landlord, who said he had not seen Diana around but that she had already paid her rent for the month.

Of course they couldn't bring the police in on it ("Maybe she just went on vacation!"), even though their emails to Diana's address went unanswered, they couldn't contact the numbers, emergency or otherwise, that she had written in her employment records, and the provincial address and previous employers she had provided them turned out to be nonexistent. Who knew? Maybe she had even given them a fake name. HR didn't look into unimportant things like character references, so the office didn't know anyone else who knew Diana beyond her name.

On Thursday night, Regina cleared out her bag and found a folded piece of paper in one of the pockets.

On Friday night she was on a bus that would take her to Heridos. She had not been home for months and her mother had been giving her hell for it. Might as well make the trip, she thought, even though, of course, she had other concerns.

When Regina unfolded the piece of paper, it showed a map on one side and two names on the other.

The paper was old, stained with coffee, and creased from being folded and unfolded repeatedly. The map was drawn and annotated with a black pen. Regina knew from internal office missives *(Kindly handle—Can you please—TY!)* that it was Diana's own handwriting.

It was a very simple map. Just shapes and lines. One big square to the right was marked *EAC FARM*. Edgar A. Cajucom was the old man's full name. An arrow pointing to the bottom of the page was marked *TOWN PROPER*, followed by several squares marked *Hospital* and *Town Hall* and *Mall/Ukay Place* and *Big Church* and *Market*. Big Church (actually the National Shrine of St. Therese) was exactly what they called the church in the town proper, because the Little Church (a small square at the top of the page) was an abandoned chapel at the edge of Ka Edgar's property. To the left of the page were rectangles and squares marked *Elementary/High School* and *Residential* and *Old Farms*. The school was a big property that had already been abandoned. Now, out-of-towners used it to shoot pre-nups and horror specials. *Residential* was composed of several squares, several houses now also abandoned. Between two *Old Farms* were two parallel lines flowing to the left of the page and beyond marked *Diversion Road to Malolos.*

At the very center of the page were five squares, with an X in one of the squares. No label, just that black X.

This didn't make sense to Regina. Everything else was correct, but there weren't any buildings near Ka Edgar's old farm.

She turned the page over and saw:

Loretta Juni

Emil Macaraeg

The names meant nothing to her.

Regina planned to only call her mother ("Did they happen to build a mall near Ka Edgar's place?"), but the moment the call connected her mother said, "So when are you coming home?"

As usual, the moment Regina stepped foot in their house her parents bombarded her with various updates about her aunts, uncles, cousins, former neighbors, and people she had not heard of before but whom her parents deemed important or interesting enough to warrant an update.

Her parents' story was the story of any other couple in Heridos, give or take one element. They were (1) in their fifties who had children in their twenties. They were (2) one of ten or more siblings. They (3) started working very young, (4) paid for their own education, and (5) worked in the city after college before returning to Heridos to raise a family.

When Regina turned seven, her father left to do blue-collar work in Taipei for five years, and her mother ran their newly opened grocery store. They saved enough money to finish the construction of the two-story house where they now lived.

Now her parents manned the store full-time, opening up at two in the morning and closing down at five in the afternoon, not changing their schedule or their lifestyle even after both of their children had finished college. They were used to hard labor. They had no use for expensive gourmet food or art films. They went to Church on Sundays, slept early, and woke up early.

Sometimes Regina wondered if they had regrets, if her father ever wished he had just stayed in Taipei, or if her mother had desires beyond raising children and living in this town, but she didn't dwell on these thoughts. In her mind her parents were always content, always happy.

"So is your brother coming home?" her father asked when they met her at the gate.

"I don't know."

"Why won't the two of you coordinate? Come home at the same time at least once so your mother will have a reason to cook me a nice dinner."

They sat down for some *caldereta*. This was Regina's favorite part of coming home, eating a meal that did not come from a can.

Her mother kept her up-to-date with her running tally of who's dead, alive, married, pregnant.

"Can you believe that Jocelyn is already turning three this year?" she said.

"Who's Jocelyn?"

"*Diyos ko,* your cousin Maia's daughter! Don't you remember?"

"Oh, is Maia the one who got pregnant in high school?"

"And she's pregnant again. With twins."

"What?"

"Well, she's married to the boy now," her father said, in a tone that seemed to say, *That should fix it!*

"Did you know that Mr. Soriano's passed on?" her mother said.

"Who's Mr. Soriano?"

"Ano ka ba, your father's friend, the *masahista?* We used to go visit him in Sto. Rosario, don't you remember? He'd give us foot massages. Your father would fall asleep during a back massage. Remember?"

"Oh, him. That's too bad."

"You remember your cousin Sonia's boyfriend, Arthur? He was your age, got hit by a truck last month."

"Yikes," Regina said, and thought, *Well, what else could you say to that?*

"He went home drunk, drove home on his motorcycle," her father said. *"Ayun."*

"Do you know what happened to Len-len?" her mother said.

"Who in the world is Len-len?" said Regina.

And so on.

Before her parents went to bed, Regina stood by their door and said, "Is there anything being built near Ka Edgar's property? A mall? A house?"

Her parents looked at each other. "I don't think so," her father replied.

"Last I heard the family's still looking for a buyer for that land," her mother said. "They had barbed wire around the old farm and the old man's house. With that big sign."

"Do you know someone named Loretta Juni?"

"I know some Junis in San Jose," said her father. "I don't remember a Loretta."

"How about Emil Macaraeg?"

"I think there's a Dr. Macaraeg at the hospital," her mother said.

"The hospital here in town?"

"Yes. Why?"

"Oh, it's nothing," Regina said, filing away this information. "Someone at work used to live here in Heridos, asked me if I knew these people."

"What's the name of your office mate?"

"Diana de Leon."

Her parents looked at each other and shrugged. "Don't know any Dianas," her mother said, and her father added, hopeful, "There are some De Leons in Sta. Rita."

Regina shrugged. "I don't know her too well, anyway. Good night."

She went to her room and called her brother. Her bedspread was new and crisp and smelled like fabric softener. Her faux-gold-gilded wooden certificate from kindergarten was still on the wall. She was surrounded by old things: old books, old photos with her old friends from high school, her old life.

"Aren't you going home?" she asked. Her brother's voice sounded tiny.

"No. I have work to finish. What's up?"

"Do you know anyone named Diana de Leon?"

"No. Who's that?"

"Never mind. Do you know that Mr. Soriano's dead?"

"Who's *that?*"

"The *masahista?* You remember him? He had this little black massager that went *brrrrrrmmmmm.*"

Luciano was laughing. *"What?"*

"That was my approximation of the sound of a massager."

Luciano laughed for a good ten seconds, and turned serious. "Sure, I remember him. That's too bad."

"How about Len-len?" she said. "You know what happened to Len-len?"

"Who the hell is Len-len?"

And so on, until she got sleepy.

The next day she got ready to look for the square marked with an X on Diana's map.

CHAPTER 4

Regina hated Heridos during the summer. In fact, she hated everything during the summer—humidity was high, temperature could peak at the mid-30s, and she could get ready for the day at an early hour and still feel like she just stepped into a sauna. She woke up on Saturday at 7 AM not because her alarm clock was blaring, but because it was too damn hot. After breakfast and a shower, she put on a pair of shorts and the thinnest shirt she could find in her cabinet. She was already damp with sweat by the time she stepped out of the gates under an umbrella.

She hailed a tricycle and chatted with the elderly driver, his leathered face crinkling as he smiled at her. She paid him, got off the tricycle, and shaded her eyes against the glare of the sun as she read the sign looming in front of her—CAJUCOM PROPERTY PRIVATE PROPERTY NO TRESPASSING—all the while wondering why she was going through all this hassle for a girl she had only known for at most two weeks.

But she was curious, and she was here, and now she trudged up the path alongside the barbed wire fence, her phone in hand. She didn't want to sweat on the paper (it could be a vital piece of evidence in the event that Diana turned up dead, a notion that Regina didn't want to entertain at length) so she took a photo of both pages last night, and kept the paper in her bag where she first found it.

The barbed wire coils were rusty; the wooden poles they were attached to pockmarked with termite holes. She traversed the length of the fence and entered a heavily wooded track. She stopped to zoom in on the image on her phone. If the map were correct, the X should be right—

Here?

Regina lowered her phone and looked around. There was nothing there, just more trees and tall grass. She walked out of the track, turned right, and walked some more—It's exercise, she told herself, wiping sweat from her face, Good cardio and shit—until she reached the chapel, the white walls now moldy and overrun with vines, like some set piece from a post-apocalyptic movie.

She turned back. Ka Edgar's house with its crooked roof was on her left. She remembered Diana's game, the fruit flies (and now she remembered the scientific name for them, *Drosophila melanogaster*), and the house in the far distance.

Should she move deeper into the wooded area?

Well, it would be cooler there, Regina thought.

She followed the wooded track and was surprised when the trees opened up into a clearing.

It took Regina several minutes of horrified staring, looking around, and checking her mental state before she finally accepted that this was happening. She had heard stories of people in town finding a path that was not there before, entering an immaculate room that had in fact burned down years ago, getting lost inside their own house—but they were stories from her childhood, and weren't they like getting held-up or kidnapped, the sort of things that happened to other people?

But it was also highly possible that she had simply missed this spot.

Yes, she thought, stepping into the clearing and making sure her phone still had a signal. *Let's go with that.*

Five steps in and the undergrowth beneath her shoes turned to grass and then to pavement. She emerged on a sidewalk. Up ahead was a collection of buildings. It was like stepping into her university right after the end of summer classes. It had the same silence, the same air of abandonment.

The buildings were gray and white, streamlined and modern, unadorned. They didn't look new but they didn't look like they had been left behind for years, like the forsaken chapel. They made Regina think of hospitals, which made her think of cemeteries, which made her think, I really shouldn't be thinking of cemeteries right now.

There were four three-story buildings arranged in a square. Regina approached the nearest and peered in through the open windows. She saw a room; empty save for a wooden desk and a couple of metal chairs. A breeze blew, and dried leaves skittered across the dusty floor, like tiny feet, or claws.

The place was making her skin crawl. She was just about to turn back when she saw a monument through the building's double doors. It was in the middle of the grassy quadrangle that the four buildings boxed in. Regina glanced back once to make sure that the path through the clearing was still there, that she still had phone signal, and walked around the building toward the huge slab of black granite. The words were carved into the stone and painted silver:

MAXIMILLIAN FORTES CENTER FOR HEREDITY
AND GENETICS
EST. 1976
A SATELLITE FACILITY
OF THE
NATIONAL INSTITUTE FOR SCIENTIFIC RESEARCH

Is this the X? she thought, placing her hand on the warm stone. She looked up, and twenty feet away was a house.

It looked just like any bungalow in town. If it were on her street, Regina wouldn't have looked twice at its peeling peach paint, its rusty red roof, its window grills, its floral print curtains, and that tiny chime hanging above the gleaming brown door. But it was a bungalow in the middle of a quadrangle of what could be a research facility.

Regina took photos of the monument and the house with her phone. The house somehow made her less afraid of the place, as though the house, despite being out of place, added a dose of normalcy to the Maximillian Fortes Center for Heredity and Genetics.

She walked over to it and was just about to reach the door when a female voice said, "Doreen?"

Regina shrieked.

"Doreen?" the voice said again. It was coming from inside the house.

The door opened and "Doreen?" the woman said, nearly crashing into Regina in her haste before shrinking back just as fast and using the door as a shield.

"You're not Doreen," she said, peeking from behind the door. The woman was older than Regina; she was perhaps in her mid-20s, pretty, but with tired eyes. These eyes were scanning Regina's face now.

"Hi," Regina said. "I'm looking for someone." She took the map from her bag and showed it to the woman.

The woman emerged from behind the door and took the piece of paper. She was wearing a dress and a shawl. A shawl in this heat? Regina felt suffocated just by looking at her.

"This is Doreen's handwriting," the woman said.

"Doreen? I know her as Diana."

"Yes." She nodded, still looking at the page. "She changes her name sometimes."

What. "She does?"

"What's your name?" the woman asked.

"Regina. And you are?"

"Florina." She said this with a sigh, as though her name made her sad. "Did Doreen say anything to you about me?"

Regina shook her head.

"She usually arrives around this time." Florina looked past her, at the granite slab, the buildings, the crackling dry leaves, as though by looking hard enough she could make Doreen appear in the landscape. She returned the paper to Regina.

Regina said, "Dian—*Doreen* is missing, actually."

Florina accepted this news with a blink.

"I work with her," Regina continued. "One day she just didn't show up for work. The office couldn't contact her. Would you know where she is?" But, really, first of all, what the fuck is your house doing here?

"She always visits me on the weekends," Florina said. "Around this time." She took a deep breath, looking off into the distance before turning back to Regina. "Would you like to come in?"

Regina sized her up. Florina seemed weird but harmless. And she was short enough to be tackled. "Sure," she said, and followed the woman through the door.

The door opened to a living room, with the kitchen, bathroom, and bedroom beyond. Between the living room and the other rooms stood two wooden shelves acting as dividers. The shelves were filled with books and various tacky knickknacks: vases, teacups, brass pitchers, miniature cars, plastic dolls, and key chains. The living room set was made of wood and rattan, reminding Regina of her grandmother's house. In the middle of the coffee table was an oil reed diffuser.

Florina saw her looking at it. "Doreen brought that for me," she said.

Regina sniffed it. It had the same minty smell as Diana's apartment.

It was cooler inside the house though there was no electric fan or air-conditioner in sight. Regina couldn't explain it.

"I have some iced tea," Florina said. Regina watched her get two glasses from the kitchen. They sat down together on the rattan chairs. The seat cushions had the same print as the curtains. Green vines, tiny red flowers.

"Have you always lived here?" Regina asked.

"Yes."

"Here," Regina said, pointing a finger to the ground for emphasis. "Here, in the middle of these buildings."

Florina massaged her neck, looking uncomfortable.

"How long have you lived here?"

"I don't—" Florina looked at her; Regina saw panic there. "I don't know."

"You don't know?"

"I've never been out of this house," she said. "I can't. I don't want to. I'm not—" She massaged her neck. "I feel safe inside. I don't go out."

"Ever?" Regina looked around the house. It was clean; there was no grime or dust on any of the knickknacks on the shelves.

"You clean and cook on your own?"

"Doreen brings me groceries every weekend. She visits every weekend."

"Do you know what these buildings are?"

Florina shot her an anguished look. *Please stop asking me questions.* But Regina couldn't stop.

"Do you know when it closed? It looks like a school."

"I don't know," she said. "I have no memory of—I feel like I've always been here."

Regina was thinking of amnesia, hostage, assault, and Stockholm Syndrome. "But Doreen is not—I mean is she the only—she's not hurting you, is she?"

Florina turned to her with a weary look. "She wouldn't hurt me."

"Are you sisters?"

"She's kind to me," Florina said, like a witness defending Diana in court.

"What's her full name?"

"I don't know."

"You don't?"

Florina looked toward the windows. "I'm not even sure what my real name is anymore," she said, in a voice so soft that Regina could hardly hear.

Florina had clearly smoked whatever it was that Diana had been smoking that night in her apartment. Regina glanced at the reed diffuser, wondered if the oil was hallucinogenic.

"You're positive she'll show up here?" she asked.

"She always shows up here." Florina said in a low tone, like how dare Regina even question this belief? Regina decided it was time to back off.

"Thank you for the iced tea," she said. "Do you have a phone?"

"No."

They stood up.

Of course, she didn't have a phone. "Can I visit you again tomorrow? I'd like to speak with Doreen." Or whatever name she goes by now.

"All right."

Regina felt strange asking, but she had to. "You're not going to disappear, are you?" she said.

"No."

"No!" She laughed out of sheer nervousness. "Of course not! It's not like you could move this house, right?"

Florina didn't return her smile.

"Right," Regina said. She opened her umbrella. "Nice seeing you."

"Wait."

Regina waited.

"Don't tell anyone about this house, all right?" Florina said.

Every ten steps or so Regina would look back and see that the house was still there. She stopped looking back when she moved out of the quadrangle and into the clearing, back to the edge of Ka Edgar's farm and the bright heat of the early-morning sun. It was not yet 9 AM. She hailed a tricycle to take her to the hospital.

CHAPTER
5

The hospital's proper name was Lolito Flores Memorial Hospital, but some letters on the sign had fallen off due to bad maintenance, and now the sign read:

LOL - - - - - - - S MEMORIAL HOSPITAL

Which didn't inspire confidence at all. It was a rundown facility with flickering lights, crumbling cork walls, old equipment, and a persistent musty smell, like a wet library. Even the santan bushes outside were covered in a thin layer of dust. They looked like they were last watered in the 1980s. *Lab Technician Wanted Apply Inside,* begged a handwritten sign taped on the glass doors. *LIBRENG TULI!* screamed another in bold red letters.

Regina entered the dim lobby and squinted at the framed directory on the wall. An E. MACARAEG (Cardiology) was listed under Room 219. She took the stairs to the second floor and walked down the hallway until she found the right number. There were four other doctors' names listed outside the door, some of them handwritten. *The Doctor Is IN,* the sign promised. There was no secretary behind the desk inside, but there was a woman sitting on one of the chairs outside the room. She was wearing a black sleeveless blouse and faded jeans, and she looked straight at Regina.

"Are you a patient of Dr. Macaraeg's?" Regina asked.

"No," the woman said. She smiled—it was a small smile, an amused smile, a smile with secrets—and said, "But you're here just in time."

"Jen?" someone said. Regina stepped through the door. A young doctor with a stethoscope around his neck and a thick sheaf of papers in his hands emerged from his clinic. "Jen, where is—oh."

"Sorry," Regina said. "No one was here."

"Yes, Jen has this tendency of leaving me alone without saying where she's going." He placed the papers on his secretary's desk and placed a glass paperweight on top of it. The name on his doctor's coat read E. Macaraeg, MD.

"Are you my 10 AM?" he said, smiling now. "You're a bit early. And you look younger than all of my patients."

"Oh, no, Doctor. I'm here to—" Regina didn't quite know where to start. She opened her bag and took out the folded piece of paper. "This will sound weird, but I work with someone named Diana de Leon, and she left this before she went missing."

"Missing?" Dr. Macaraeg unfolded the paper.

"Well, we're not sure. She probably just went on vacation. My name's Regina, by the way."

Dr. Macaraeg studied the page. "Is this my name?" He looked up, confused. Regina shrugged.

"Let's go talk inside," he said, and gestured toward his clinic. Regina sat on a chair in front of his desk. A life-sized anatomical model of the human heart, the kind children could disassemble, sat on his table. Its valves were numbered. Regina tried to recall her Biology lessons. Inferior vena cava. Left ventricle. Pulmonary valve.

Dr. Macaraeg sat down behind his desk with a grunt. "What did you say your friend's name was again?"

"Diana de Leon. Maybe she was a patient?"

"I don't recall ever seeing a patient by that name."

"How about Doreen?"

The doctor paused for a moment then shook his head.

"Do you know anyone named Loretta Juni?"

"No," he said. He pointed at the page. "What about this map, then?"

"I don't know, Doctor," she said.

"That's Ka Edgar's farm, right?"

"You know the place?"

"I was born and raised here. Are these supposed to be buildings?"

Regina remembered the empty buildings again, the grassy quadrangle, and felt a chill. Did she really see that just an hour ago?

"Maybe. But there's nothing on that property but his house."

The doctor tapped a finger on the page—once, twice, thrice—and returned it to Regina. He looked at her, but Regina knew he wasn't really looking at her. He looked bothered.

"This is really strange."

"I know."

"You said she was missing?"

"Or on vacation," Regina said. "We're not sure. We haven't told the police."

"Does anyone else know about her note?"

She shook her head.

"Why didn't you tell your office about it?"

That's a very good question. "That's a very good question," she said. Because she gave it to me? Because it felt like she wanted me to figure it out? "I wasn't sure she was the one who wrote it until I left the city."

"And now you're sure?"

Regina shrugged. She didn't want to tell him about Florina, and his questions were making her uncomfortable.

The doctor opened a small cardboard box on his table. It coughed up several business cards. He chose one from the mess and handed it to her.

"Can you update me about this?" he said. Regina looked at the card and inserted it in her wallet.

Two women were waiting outside. The older one, wearing thick glasses, straightened up and said, "Doctor—"

"Jen," Dr. Macaraeg said with a sigh. "Where in the world have you been?"

She gestured toward the other woman, who was holding onto the strap of her shoulder bag so tightly her knuckles were white.

"I'm so sorry, Doctor," Jen said. "Your 10 AM is—"

"Clara, is it?" He shook the woman's hand. The woman seemed jumpy. "Please take a seat for a minute, I just need to make a call. Regina—"

"Can I ask you a question?" Regina said.

Dr. Macaraeg, who was already halfway in his clinic, stepped back out. "I have a million of those now because of this friend of yours, but you go ahead."

"Would you know if there was a research facility built here in Heridos? Say, a facility for researching genetics?"

39

"Have you seen this hospital?" he said, and Regina had to laugh. "We don't even have a decent 2D Echo machine. If there was such a facility here in town, I would personally ask the sponsors to donate to Flores."

"Of course," she said. "Thank you, Doctor."

Regina expected to see the woman in black outside, but the chairs were empty.

CHAPTER 6

Regina bought a cheese sandwich and a cup of coffee in the hospital cafeteria (located in the basement, and, despite all appearances, sold decent food) and headed outside to a nearby computer shop. It was a narrow room with two rows of computers, smelling of burnt wires, potato chips, and sweat. Gamer funk. A handful of grade school boys in a corner of the room wore headphones and cursed at each other.

"No cursing or I'll throw you out," said the man seated at the main computer, behind a tall desk with a ceramic *maneki neko* figurine beckoning with her paw. The man issued his warning without much conviction. He looked half-asleep. "Number seven's free," he said to her, and she sat down on the Monobloc chair in front of Computer Number 7.

She took a bite of her sandwich and typed the URL for the website of the National Institute for Scientific Research. About the Institute (*established during the Commonwealth years with the help of American scientists* blah blah *is the nation's research agency providing support for the Departments of Health, Science and Technology, and Agriculture* blah blah *primarily located in Quezon City with five provincial centers* blah blah blah). News. Research & Publications. Training Opportunities. Locations. Contact Us.

Regina clicked on "Locations" and studied the drop-down menu. Quezon City. Cebu. Davao. Baguio. Vigan. No listing for Heridos.

There was no exact match for "Maximillian Fortes Center for Heredity and Genetics", but there were results for "Maximillian Fortes." On top of the page, under Image Results, were: a black-and-white photo of a Caucasian man, a toddler, and, for some damn reason, a screenshot from *Face/Off* of Nicholas Cage smiling maniacally. Regina rolled her eyes, and tried adding "genetics" and "heredity" to the search.

Among the top ten results was a very short Wiki article ("This medical article is a stub.") on Maximillian Fortes, a graduate of the University of Santo Tomas and Johns Hopkins University, who did significant research work on tropical diseases. He was born in 1880 in Manila; he died in Baltimore, Maryland in 1955. The article had a single source, an obituary published in a medical journal. Regina clicked the link.

The article opened as a PDF file. *Maximillian Fortes, MD*, read the top of the page, followed by two long paragraphs detailing Dr. Fortes's academic and medical achievements. *Fortes's research took him to all parts of the world, civilized and uncivilized*, a sentence went, which made Regina raise an eyebrow. Civilized *and* uncivilized, huh? What a visionary. What a trailblazer. Right before the second paragraph was the sentence, *He was survived by his only daughter, Dorothea.*

Dorothea Fortes was born in 1948 to a Fil-American mother, who was Maximillian Fortes's second wife. Regina couldn't find any information about the wives. The younger Fortes was a neuropsychiatrist and a surgeon who also studied genetics, perhaps to honor her dead father. Regina found a photo of Dorothea (captioned "Thea Fortes, MD"), published in a newspaper a month or so ago. She was cutting a ribbon for the opening of a clinic in Malolos.

She would be in her late 60s now. Retired. Dorothea—Thea—looked fantastic in the photo, with high cheekbones and big hair. Regina wondered if she lived in the province.

Regina finished her sandwich and coffee, and logged out. She stood behind the counter to wait for her change, and noticed the phonebook sitting beside the phone.

"Can I borrow this?" she asked, and leafed through it. It should have occurred to her earlier to check, but the last time she looked through a phonebook that was not in a cell phone was—well, she couldn't even remember the last time she did that.

There was a Loretta Juni in Barangay San Jose right in Heridos, and a Dorothea Fortes in Sapang Malaki, Paombong. Regina took out her phone and snapped a photo of the contact details.

And that's when she remembered: she took a photo of the house and the monument inside the research facility that, as far as Dr. Macaraeg and the Internet were concerned, did not exist.

She swiped back. The photos were not there.

CHAPTER 7

Regina waited for a tricycle under a Duhat tree in front of the hospital near the road. The tree was bloated, in season. Some of the overripe fruit had already fallen to the ground, stepped on and stamped into the cement, leaving behind gutted white flesh, wide arcs of crimson and black stains like a wine spill.

She was not too concerned about the photos. Her phone was old and its memory settings sometimes go wonky. But. Still. She felt like she was living inside one of her grandmother's stories. *Once there was a young girl who found four buildings and a quadrangle, which was either a hallucinatory product of heatstroke or a place that actually exists. Though it probably doesn't? Then she found courage or love or something. The end. Next: The Boy Who Cried Wolf.*

"Excuse me?"

Regina jumped in surprise, and the woman who appeared in front of her jumped too, like a delayed shadow.

"I'm sorry," she said. "I didn't mean to startle you." She held onto her bag for dear life. Regina glanced at her white knuckles and remembered her.

"You were at Dr. Macaraeg's clinic earlier," Regina said.

"Yes." The woman smiled, as though overjoyed that she

didn't have to go through the painful process of putting herself in context. "Clara. I've been meaning to talk to you."

A tricycle stopped by the tree. It felt rude to leave Clara in the middle of her explanation, so Regina just shook her head. The tricycle sped away to another passenger, and Regina said, "Why?"

Clara was staring at her shoes, at the Duhat fruit stains on the ground. She spoke haltingly, stopping every three words or so. "You asked the doctor about a facility here, a research facility for genetics?"

Regina turned to her, moved a bit closer. "Yes?"

"Why were you asking about it?" Clara said. Her voice dropped to a whisper. "Did you see it?"

In the pause between her two questions Regina was already thinking of an acceptable answer. *I heard about it from a friend,* for example, but then Clara would ask, *Which friend?* and Regina didn't want to get into it right now, and anyway, *who is this girl?*

But then: *Did you see it?*

"What do you—"

"You saw it," Clara said, her eyes filling up with tears. "Please tell me you saw it."

Another tricycle stopped. Regina looked at Clara, thinking.

"Are you getting in or not?" the driver asked, just when Regina was about to speak. She felt like punching the driver in the face, but she just shook her head.

"Does the name Maximillian Fortes mean anything to you?" she asked, and Clara gasped, sending Regina into panic, thinking she was in pain. But Clara was smiling.

"I knew it!" she said, wiping tears away from the corner of her eyes. "I knew it. After all these years. I am not losing my mind."

Regina felt like she was losing her mind. "Would you like to sit down somewhere and talk about it?"

Clara would very much love to sit down and talk about it. As they walked out of the shade, Regina felt a prickle on the back of her neck. She looked up, the movement sudden and sharp, turning her head like a child sensing danger.

She thought she saw something stirring in the branches.

They took a tricycle together to the town mall. Beside her, Clara kept her hands on her knees, squeezing them, as though she were in pain and trying her best and hardest not to scream. Regina looked away, not wanting to get into more awkward small talk.

"Mall" was too generous a word to describe the building where they alighted. There was only one proper shop—a school-supplies-and-used-books store that was so old it still sold floppy disk cleaners—while everything else was sold in small stalls: secondhand clothing, cell phones, computer parts. There were some restaurants, a couple of offices for the electric company and the water company, and two banks, one rural and one major.

They went to a fast food restaurant rip-off—Jollibelle or something—and sat in a booth. Clara ordered coffee; Regina got a glass of water. Clara took a deep breath and said, "Where did you first hear about it?"

Regina told her about Diana, and showed her the page with the map and the names.

"Do you recognize the names?" she asked.

"No," Clara said. "Your friend's name is?"

"Diana de Leon," she replied. "Or Doreen."

"You're not sure?"

Regina shrugged. "How about you? How do *you* know about the center?"

"You mean, how do I know about this and no one else does." Clara's smile did not reach her eyes.

"Yes. Yes, why is that?"

"I've been asking that question for as long as I can remember," Clara said. "I've told my family about it, my doctors, I've asked around. I even went to the town hall and pestered people about it. No one knew what I was talking about." She looked at her. "You're the first person I heard mention it."

"What do you know about it?"

Clara looked away, bit her fingernails. "There are gaps in my memory," she said, and began talking in earnest. "Big gaps. Though my therapist—I used to have a therapist, of course there weren't any here because people here didn't believe in shrinks, so I had to go to Manila to meet this lady but after a couple of months my sister refused to pay for her services because all the talking wasn't really helping so she said I should just stick with my medication—anyway—sorry—and this is my *younger* sister we're talking about, she's always been my parents' favorite—sorry—anyway—my therapist thinks what I have are false memories." Clara looked at Regina, and the look on her face broke Regina's heart. "But they're not. I know they're not. And I'm thinking, if I can't even believe myself, who should I believe?"

"What do you remember?"

"Doctors," Clara said. "Or I think they're doctors. Lab coats. I remember the full name of the center because I remember it was engraved on—"

"Black graphite."

"—the floor," Clara finished. "Black graphite? I don't remember that."

Regina nodded. "Okay, go on. Never mind what I said."

"I remember," Clara said, "steel railings. White walls. The

sound that gloves make when you snap them on your wrist. I was young, maybe ten years old or younger, and I was sitting on a chair and my parents were talking to someone. I remember they signed something, and the next time I saw those documents again they were redacted."

"Redacted."

"They looked like reports. They were typewritten, but a lot of the passages were crossed out with a black marker. I remember a thick black line on top of the page and I remember *knowing* without a doubt that that was my name they had crossed out."

"How old are you now, Clara?"

"Twenty-nine."

She was her brother's age. "So, this happened," she said, "two decades ago?"

They sat still for a moment. Regina took a sip of water.

Clara said, "These memories, you know, they were just *images*. I can't tell you when or where exactly they happened. But I have one memory that was at least crystal-clear."

Regina folded her hands on top of the table and waited.

"Dead children," she said. "A lot of dead children. Twenty or thirty. And there were these people arranging them in concentric circles, three or four rows deep. Standing in the center, surrounded by all these bodies, was a tall person whose face I couldn't see very clearly."

Regina was chilled by this until, a few seconds later, she thought, *okay this is a bit insane.*

"Where is this?"

"On a field outside the buildings." Clara had begun crying again, and now she wiped her tears with a piece of tissue. "I dream about them often. In the dreams, sometimes, they're covered in blood. Or they're decapitated. Or I'm a part of them, and I could feel myself being dragged by the arm across the grass and being turned on my side so I could be in position."

"Who were the people dragging these children?"

"I don't know."

"Who were these children?"

"I think they were with me," Clara said. "In the Center."

"But what did they do to you in the Center?" Regina asked. "What was it for?" And a question she couldn't bring herself to ask: Why were you saved?

"I don't know," Clara said again, and ended up sobbing into her coffee cup.

Regina gave her a minute to compose herself.

"Maximillian Fortes is a real person, you know," she said, slowly, as though afraid the revelation would break Clara.

But Clara nodded and said, "I know. And I know he has a living descendant, a daughter. Dorothea. I went as far as standing outside the gate of her house, but I just couldn't make myself ring the doorbell. I did try calling the Institute, because I remember the Center was connected to the Institute. They said they've never had an organization with that name, though they do conduct research on genetics and heredity. I asked them if they employ Dorothea Fortes, and they said the doctor used to be connected to the Institute but now she has her own small private practice." She huffed in exasperation. "I don't understand why this is happening. They can't all be lying to me."

"Do you recall the exact location of the center?" Regina asked.

"No. All I remember was it was within town."

Regina pointed at the map. "I went looking for this X," she said.

Clara looked at her, thinking, then her eyes widened. "It was the Center."

Regina described what she saw, but did not mention Florina or her house.

"I took a photo of the place," Regina said. "But now the photos aren't in my phone."

Clara stirred her coffee. She had not sipped a drop. "What does it mean?"

"Do you remember any names? Anything mentioned while you were in the Center?"

Clara shook her head. "If I did, I would have followed it up the moment I remembered it," she said. "I want to get to the bottom of this. Especially now, when you just proved that I *wasn't* making it all up."

"Unless I'm also hallucinating."

Clara laughed. "You look all right." She turned serious. "Listen, can we—" She touched her hair, scratched her cheek with a finger. "Can you—can you show me where it is? I want to see it with my own eyes."

Regina glanced at the clock on the wall. It was high noon. Her mother would like her back for lunch. And she didn't want to walk on the old man's farm in this heat.

"How about later? Late afternoon? I feel like taking a nap."

"Yes," Clara said, eager. "Sure. Where I should I meet you?"

"Ka Edgar's farm. Let me get your number."

After they exchanged numbers, Regina said, "Clara, are you sick?"

Clara's look was sharp, and Regina became suddenly aware of her horrible phrasing. "I mean, your heart. Sorry. You were at Dr. Macaraeg earlier."

"Oh," Clara said. She smiled, relieved. "Nothing major. Arrhythmia. But I have other problems. Anxiety, mostly." She crossed her arms. "You know something? I always carry those perfumes that come in glass bottles. Never the plastic ones.

Glass. I would think, if someone attacked me, I could smash the glass and stab him in the neck with the jagged edge. I would think, the horrible days in my life, they have yet to come. Both of my parents are still alive. So is my sister. My parents don't like me, you see. I know that sounds melodramatic, but I'm not exaggerating. My sister, my *younger* sister whom they adore, is working as a bank manager in the city. She doesn't like me either. But they're family. They're the only people I could turn to. And their deaths are still waiting for me, just up ahead, and I know, whatever pain I'm feeling right now, it's small compared to the pain that's still to come." Her eyes filled with tears, and the tears spilled over, shiny like crystal drops. "This is how I always think. This is how I live my life. It's not a very enjoyable life. I make up my own monsters." She tried to smile. "At least I know I did not make this one up."

Regina, who was not a hugger, felt like hugging Clara. But all she could do was smile back at her. "I'll see you later, Clara," she said.

CHAPTER 8

After having lunch with her parents (*sinigang, laing,* and hot cocoa from melted *tablea*—Regina could have cried with gratitude), Regina sat on her bed. There were three missed calls from her brother. Strange. He probably wanted her to check a book he had left behind in his room, which was usually the reason he called her whenever she was back at the house. She sent him a quick text ("Whts up") and took note of Dr. Fortes's contact details.

An elderly woman answered on the fourth ring. "Dr. Fortes's clinic." She sounded chipper. Chummy grandma, a cheek pincher.

"Hello."

"Yes, this is Irma, the doctor's secretary. How can I help you, dear?"

"I was wondering what time the doctor opens her clinic. Does she focus on psychiatry?"

Irma laughed. "Not a lot of folks in Paombong seek a psychiatrist, though that's the doctor's specialization. She's known as a GP here, general practitioner."

"I see."

"We open 9 AM and close around 5 PM. But that's not strict. Most of her consultations are by appointment. We're open when someone comes in. Otherwise she just stays in the house and reads. Would you like to set an appointment?"

"Walk-ins are okay?"

"Of course."

"I think we'll just walk in tomorrow. I don't know yet what time we can come in."

"You call when you have the time, dear. Or, you know, just drop by. She'll be here."

"Yes," she said. "Thank you."

Regina called her brother next. "What's up? Did you need me to look for a book?"

"Oh hey Reg."

"You called me three times."

"I just wanted to check up on you. Did you go out?"

"Just to the computer shop."

"Oh, okay. How are the parents?"

"They're okay." Regina frowned. "What's going on?"

"What do you mean?"

"Why are you checking up on me? You're not dying, are you?" Regina could hear a whooshing sound. "Are you driving?"

"No. I'm at my apartment. Why would I be driving?"

"You're weird."

"*You're* weird."

Regina lay on her bed. "I have a question."

"Mm."

"Does the name Maximillian Fortes mean anything to you?"

Luciano was quiet for a moment. "Sounds like a Bond villain."

"He does, doesn't he. Do you know anyone named—" Regina shook her head. Why does she even bother, the answer would be no. She had asked her parents about Fortes, and they just looked at her with a frown. "Never mind."

"What?" her brother said.

"It's nothing. Look, I'll take a nap."

"Okay. Bye-bye."

Regina went out to get the electric fan from Luciano's room, and pointed the two electric fans at her bed. She set her alarm and fell asleep almost immediately.

Regina couldn't breathe. She was getting ready to panic, until she felt her swinging arms, the pain in her calves. The realization came: she was running, and had been doing so for hours. She could feel sharp rocks under her feet, then grass, then wet, warm blood as thick as engine oil.

Scene change. Diana was standing beside her. The sky was overcast, and they were standing on a sidewalk waiting for the light to change. A red DON'T WALK sign blinked on the display on the other side of the street. Diana and Regina remained where they were, even though the street looked completely deserted. They could have crossed it to the other side in less than ten seconds.

"There you are," she told Diana. "Everyone's been looking for you."

"Everyone?"

"Well. Just me, mostly. Where the hell have you been?"

Diana didn't reply. Black birds flew overhead. Regina watched them. When she lowered her gaze the sign now said WALK in green letters.

"Aren't we going to cross now?" she asked. Diana looked at her with sad eyes. On the other side of the street, on either side of the post with the traffic sign, stood a man and a woman. The woman was wearing a white dress. She had long black hair. The man was wearing black pants, and a black blazer over a white shirt. They looked like they came from a wedding. Regina couldn't see their faces. The woman lifted a finger and Regina felt a breeze ruffle her hair. The man raised his hand as though to wave, and the clouds parted, revealing the sun.

"Isn't it high time you explained yourself?" the man said, but it was to Regina that Diana replied: "Not yet."

When Regina woke up it was 4 PM, and her clothes and pillows were soaked with sweat.

She met up with Clara at the old man's farm at around 5 PM. The sky was a beautiful bronze color. Clara was wearing the same shirt, and her hair looked rumpled.

"Hi," she said, her voice shaking.

"It's 5 PM and it's still hot," Regina said, hoping to calm her with worthless weather talk. "Unbelievable."

They began to walk. "I have an idea, Clara."

Clara's mind was somewhere far away. She was wringing her hands. Regina could see her trying to pull herself back to the here and now. "Yes?"

"Let's go see Dr. Fortes tomorrow," she said. "Let's pretend you're a patient."

Clara smiled. "I wouldn't need to pretend, really." Her smile disappeared. "I don't know, I—"

"I'll be there," Regina said. "I'll ask the questions. Meanwhile, think of an alias."

"Won't they ask for ID?" She shook her head. "No, I'll tell her my name. I'll check if that will get a reaction from her."

"See? You're thinking ahead already."

They walked on in silence. An easy stroll, except that Clara moved as if she had ants in her shirt. When they reached the trees, Clara erupted in a high-pitched scream: "It's not here. Nothing's here. I don't—"

"Clara? Breathe. Relax." But she was right. There was nothing here. They were standing at the point where the clearing was supposed to be. Regina walked forward, even though she already knew. She was there just this morning. She was not mistaken. The path had disappeared.

"Son of a bitch!" she said, and saw that Clara was looking at her with mounting terror in her eyes.

"Clara, listen. I really saw it. I did not make it up." She pointed at a spot in the trees. "There was a clearing right here just this morning!"

"I believe you," Clara said. She combed through her hair with her fingers, a nervous tic. "There's something *wrong* with this place."

Regina kicked at a weed. "This place is driving me *nuts*."

"It doesn't want to reveal itself," Clara said, and glanced at Regina. "I sound crazy right now, don't I?"

"I've heard the same stories from my grandmother, Clara."

"I had a great-aunt who said when she was a girl, she would see a man wearing a *salakot* walking through these rice fields. Back when this area still had rice. She said some of the farmers saw him too, and they told her the appearance of this man was a sign of good harvest." She paused. "Of course, he wasn't really a man."

"Of course!" Regina sighed, threw up her hands. "Spirit stories are a dime a dozen here."

"It's getting dark," Clara said.

"I'm so sorry, Clara."

Clara looked at the trees, the old man's house. "It's not your fault."

They walked to the road in heavy silence without looking back, and got on a tricycle. The temperature dropped as
dusk settled. It got dark quickly in Heridos. It was something
Regina had forgotten, having studied and lived for years in the
city, with its perpetual lights, its constant stream of people. In
Heridos, especially in the Poblacion where they lived, you could
tell what time it was based on the number of people out on the
roads: a lot from dawn to midmorning, and maybe one or two
loafers during siesta time and in the evening. By 10 PM, the
roads would be completely empty. They didn't need a curfew;
the town imposed it on itself.

Regina heard a soft thump behind her. When she looked
back, she saw something dark and flimsy pass in front of her
eyes and fall back, like black gauze.

"Did you see that?" she said, frightened.

"What?" Clara said.

But there was nothing behind them, just the road, and a car
a long way back. Out-of-towners.

"I thought I saw something."

"Is my anxiety rubbing off on you? I have pills."

Regina turned to her and realized that Clara was joking.
She laughed.

The next day, she and Clara met in front of the town hall
and got on a jeep to Malolos. They got down in Paombong.
Regina followed Clara's lead. They walked past a couple of
houses with shuttered windows, past a table filled with jars of
Paombong vinegar, the pungent smell announcing the product
ahead of the hand-painted sign: SUKA O TUBA 4SALE. They
walked past a house with a gate decorated with colorful sketches of fish and sea creatures. A huge sign said Glass bottom boat

maker inquire inside. *Vannamei (Whiteleg shrimp)*, one label read, accompanied by a sketch of a shrimp.

"Vannamei," Regina said. "That's cute. Sounds like the name of a girl band."

For a long moment Clara didn't reply. Then she said, "You're thinking of Vanna Vanna."

Regina laughed, feeling a little unhinged. Look at us, two girls having a ball.

"Thank you for doing this," Clara said. "Why are you, though?"

"What? Doing this?" Regina said, and realized in that moment (though the thought was still shapeless, incomplete) that she was no longer snooping to find out what happened to Diana. She wasn't really even doing this for Clara. She was doing it for herself.

The doctor's gated property had a short walkway from the gate to the front door, crowded on both sides by pink and white bougainvillea bushes. The flowers were so thick and the branches hung so low that Regina felt a little suffocated. There was a yellowing sign on the wall of the house that said DOROTHEA FORTES, MD, and below that, in smaller font, *General Practitioner*. On the front door was a message written on bond paper: *Clinic entrance at the back.*

They went to the back, where they found an open door that led to a waiting area. There were four people on the couch: a mother and (presumably) her son, a middle-aged woman with sparkling diamond jewelry, and an old man with a cane already half-asleep. Irma, wearing a pair of glasses on a silver chain, was sitting behind a desk, having some tea.

"How can I help you, dear?" she said.

Clara was given a paper attached to a clipboard to fill out. "You still want to do this?" Regina said. Clara replied by writing her name on the page.

A woman got out of the clinic and the mother and son got in. There was a burst of happy greetings. *Doktoraaaa, how are you?* They were followed by the woman with the diamond jewelry. When the old man shuffled through the door, Regina stood up and looked at the photos on the walls. They were mostly event photos, Thea Fortes wining and dining. There was a photo of her taken in a studio, her hands folded on an armrest, her smile small and cunning. She looked like Greta Garbo.

A bit high up on one wall was a small black-and-white photo of men, some of them Caucasian-looking, posing in front of a building. On either side of them were policemen in uniform. Everybody looked grim and serious. At the bottom of the photo was a label in white letters, *1906. Scientists from the Philippine Biological Laboratory. National Bilibid Prisons.*

1906.

Bilibid.

In 1906, an American director of the Philippine Biological Laboratory infected Bilibid inmates with cholera.

Something clicked.

"Miss Irma," Regina said, "is Doktora Fortes's father in this photo?"

Clara looked up, but didn't stand to get a closer look. The secretary squinted. "Is this the little photo at the Bilibid? Yes, he's with that group. He's very young in that photo, 'no? Spiffy looking young man."

When their turn was called, Regina went over to Clara, and felt her arms stiffen. "Regina," she said. "I'm not sure I—"

"Don't worry," Regina whispered. "This won't take long."

They walked through the door. Dr. Fortes had a Jackie O. bob, lined with gray. Her lids were painted deep ochre. She was writing on a page with a gold pen, making her diamond bracelets jangle. The frames of her glasses were also made of gold. Several points of her glinted: pen, bracelet, glass frames. Regina imagined the diamond-studded woman who came before her as the doctor's *alahera*. "Hello, dears," she said, smiling, and now her eyes glinted too. "Please have a seat."

She continued writing. Clara was as stiff as a board. "Come on," Regina urged, and got her to sit down.

Dr. Fortes took the clipboard. Perfume wafted from her skin. "Okay, Clara," she said, looking at her. "What seems to be the problem?"

Clara's breathing was very audible, as though she were hyperventilating. "You don't know me?" she said.

Dr. Fortes looked at her, then at Regina. "Am I supposed to?"

"My name," Clara said. "My name doesn't sound familiar?"

"Are you all right, dear?"

Clara covered her mouth and heaved.

"Oh!" the doctor said, pointing to her right. "The bathroom's over—"...."

Clara made it to the toilet in time. She vomited violently. Regina, not knowing what to do, lingered by the door with the doctor.

Clara washed her mouth and face at the sink, tore off some paper towels, wiped her face. Without another word she walked briskly out of the room, slamming the door behind her.

"Um," Regina said.

"Well, then," Dr. Fortes said. "I hope your friend comes back."

They walked back to her desk. "Actually," Regina said. "I wanted to ask you a few questions."

"Oh? Are you ill, as well?"

"Your father was part of the Bilibid experiment?"

The doctor locked eyes with her for several moments, took a deep breath, and sat back on her chair. She opened a drawer, took out a packet of cigarettes and a lighter. "Smoke?"

"No," Regina said, taken aback.

Dr. Fortes rolled her chair back and opened a window. Her window overlooked a garden, a huge chunk of the blue sky. She lit a cigarette, took a drag. "I thought I'd gotten rid of you people years ago."

"What do you mean?"

"You're not one of those activists?" she said. "So, what is this, just a personal interest?"

"Activists?"

"Most of them were based in the US." Dr. Fortes blew smoke out the window, tapped her cigarette on the windowsill. "When Clinton apologized for the Tuskegee experiment, they were the ones who raised a ruckus. Why won't the US apologize for Bilibid, they asked. Bleeding hearts, all of them! Fighting for the rights of murderers and rapists they would have stoned to death anyway if given the chance."

How sure was she that they were indeed serious criminals? It was 1906. Regina wasn't a history expert, but she knew Spain ceded the Philippine Islands to the Americans at around that time, which led to a war between the Philippines and the US. Those "criminals" could very well be the Filipino revolutionaries thrown into prison by the American soldiers.

"So," Regina said, "you were in favor of the Tuskegee experiment?"

"What happened in Tuskegee was a mess," Dr. Fortes said. "The Bilibid inmates gave their consent. That's what they forget. The inmates *agreed* to it."

But Diana said they *didn't* agree to it. "Why would anyone agree to be infected?"

"Oh, sweetheart. The pill you take to keep headaches at bay? The cream you slather on your wounds? They were products of clinical trials. People sign on to join these trials for money. Maybe for science. But mostly for money. They sign on to knowing that some of the trials might end up with them nursing a skin burn, or with their death. If you ask me, if you can successfully do the experiment on an animal, just use an animal. But people are harping on this cruelty-free bullshit. Really, would you rather have dead babies than dead mice? If you ask me, I'd rather have the dead mice."

"But you can't always use animals."

"Aye, there's the rub. Sooner or later you'd need to use a human subject. Otherwise we would just release the drug to the general population and hope for the best. 'It worked on the rat inside the lab, so this should work on you! Call this number in case of anaphylaxis!'"

"The inmates weren't paid, though."

Dr. Fortes laughed. "Are you seriously concerned with the welfare of these degenerates? Seriously? In your heart of hearts. If given the choice between a criminal and your mother, to whose arm should we inject the syringe filled with cholera?"

"Why should those be the only choices?" Regina asked. "I don't want to think one person's inferior to me."

The doctor smiled around her cigarette. "But you have," she said. "Several times in your life. If a cashier at a fast-food restaurant can't get your orders straight you're already judging her in your head. Slow. Dumb. Idiot. At least once you've stood in front of a food server and thought, I am better than this worthless piece of shit. Admit it. You have."

Regina didn't reply.

"When you listen to the evening news and hear the anchor say a college graduate died, you think, Oh, that poor girl. She had her life ahead of her. The things she could have done. The world is dimmer without her. When a homeless person dies, what do you feel? Nothing. I doubt his death would even get reported. And I'm sure a lot of people will say, Good riddance."

"That sounds a bit cruel."

"It is pragmatic," the doctor said. "Sentiment can only get you so far."

"So, you think some people are born to be a burden on the rest."

"Aren't they?" she said. "Pregnant women now have the choice to undergo screening, to check if the fetus in their uterus has Down's, or if it will be born blind or deaf or with its brain exposed."

"But they do it so they can be ready for whatever might come next."

"And if they choose to abort the fetus, will you judge them?"

Regina felt tired. "No," she said. "It's their choice."

"If you find out that someone you know has genes that carry a fatal disease that she will surely pass on to her children," the doctor said, "would you encourage her to still have children?"

"That choice is not for me to make. It's her life."

"And if she chooses to go ahead and get pregnant, knowing the child will lead a painful life, won't you judge her? Won't you think she is selfish, imposing this child on the world?"

"But it's her life."

"We're all connected, dear. It's never only her life. That child will undergo treatments, ask for donations from people, and use government funds. Wouldn't you think everyone would be better off if she just had a hysterectomy?"

Regina felt violated. She felt like she would start crying any second now. "If we lived during the Holocaust, we would both be dead."

"Hitler was a madman," the doctor said. "He discriminated based on religion and skin and eye color and sexual orientation. I'm talking about independence and productivity. If you are able to live independently as a productive member of society, then we're all good. Otherwise—" She shrugged. "The best thing parents could do with their subpar children—"

Subpar? Regina thought, the word a scream inside her head.

"—if they choose not to sterilize them, is to donate them to science. At least, in that way, they will be able to help the rest of the population."

Who are you to prescribe what is good and what is bad for the world? If you write the criteria, where do you start and where do you stop? The eugenics movement discriminated against people with *epilepsy*. Against people who are *depressed*. Should Clara be sterilized, is that what she was saying?

But Regina bit her tongue and tried to return to her original plan, which was to ask, "Did the Institute ever build a center named after your father?"

The doctor raised her eyebrows. "Where did you hear that? That was an old plan. An old, old plan, circa Marcos years. In the end, the Institute decided to just include it within their premises in QC, instead of building a separate center and hiring more people. Budget and logistics problems, all that."

"It was never built?"

"Afraid so." Her voice turned wistful. "I still have the blue-prints somewhere. We were supposed to have four buildings. A quadrangle."

Regina glanced over her shoulder. "Sorry my friend ran out like that. I don't think she's coming back."

"Anxiety problems," Dr. Fortes said, and killed her cigarette on the windowsill. She smiled at Regina. "Come back any time."

Regina found Clara sitting in the town plaza several blocks away. There were a group of young boys playing ball on the basketball court, their flip-flops slapping on the pavement. Clara sat in the shade, on a stone bench, crying into her hands. Regina bought a bottle of cold water from a store nearby and gave it to her.

"Dr. Fortes scared the life out of me," Regina said. "I don't blame you for getting out of there."

Clara took a drink of water and said, "I remember her smell."

"Her smell?"

"Her perfume. I remember her. She was there."

Regina sat down beside her. "She said the center was never built. I don't think she was lying. She was a *very* forthcoming person."

They sat in silence for a while. Someone scored on the court. The boys cheered.

"It was never built?" Clara said. "What does that mean?"

Regina didn't know what to say.

"If this is just the tip of the iceberg," Clara said, "and this is what it's doing to me, then I'd rather it remained submerged, you know?"

"You don't want to—"

Horrible, hiccupping sobs from Clara. "I don't want to remember anymore."

They fell silent. "I understand," Regina said after a moment. She placed a hand on her arm. "Let's get you home."

Back at her parents' house, Regina fell asleep again in the haze of the quiet, sweltering afternoon, and once again dreamt that she was running.

This time, though, someone was holding her hand.

CHAPTER
9

Later in the day, Regina went back to the old man's farm alone, and sure enough when she got to the spot in the trees, the clearing was there. She couldn't tell why this didn't surprise her. She walked to the quadrangle, and there stood the buildings and the graphite slab and Florina's house, appearing the way they did the first time she saw them.

She didn't go straight to Florina. She went to the building on her right and entered the doors. There was a huge semicircular desk up ahead. On either side of her were groups of plump chairs arranged around tables. So, this was the lobby. The waiting area. Regina looked down. On the marble floor, barely visible, was the name of the center encircling its logo. Regina was stepping on it, and she couldn't make out the symbols. Eroded by foot traffic, the logo on the floor probably predated the monument outside. So Clara remembered the sign on the floor, but not the black graphite. At some point in the Center's history, Management must have thought what they did was important enough to merit a monument.

For an hour, Regina explored the four buildings, her steps echoing in the empty hallways. Sunlight streamed through open windows. She saw clinics, offices, laboratories that still housed equipment. Microscopes, shelves with glass jars and petri dishes, trolleys, test tubes, larger machines whose names Regina did not know. She saw several rooms with the same configuration—a single bed, one chair, and no windows. These rooms had signs like *Examination Room 1* or *Quarantine 1*. She saw at least four wards that had upwards of ten beds placed side by side. There were rooms in the basement that had at most thirty beds. She saw a room that had a sign that said *Records*, but the room was empty save for lockers, file cabinets, and shelves. Same as the room marked *Pharmacy*. She couldn't find a clue anywhere about what they did in those buildings. It was as if the Center were an insect that died in the trees, and what was left behind was its empty, useless shell.

When she knocked on the door of Florina's house, she emerged with her arms up to her elbows covered with soapsuds. She wiped them on her apron. "Oh, it's you," Florina said. She sounded disappointed.

"Doreen still hasn't—?"

"No."

Regina sat on the sofa while Florina made sandwiches. Florina was doing her laundry in the sink. Wrung clothes sat on top of each other in a teetering pyramid. After a few minutes, Florina walked to the living room, carrying sandwiches and drinks on a wooden tray. The design on the plates matched the coasters of the glasses. Florina sat on the chair across the sofa and took a very small bite of her sandwich, as though she were eating just to be polite. Regina drank her iced tea in big, hungry gulps and lowered the glass on the table.

"What is this place, Florina?"

Florina took another small bite of her sandwich. Her eyes looked frightened. She averted her gaze.

"I spoke to someone who knew about the Center. She said this was never built. So, what is this? Someone's dream?"

Still no reply.

"But I also spoke to someone who remembered being in here. At some point this place actually existed." Regina took a deep breath to calm herself. "I brought her here with me yesterday, but we couldn't find the entrance. Why is that?"

"Because you were with someone who wasn't supposed to see."

"How come *I* could see it?"

Florina glanced at her, a quick glimpse, then looked down. "Doreen gave you the map in her own handwriting."

"So, what—is Doreen this place's caretaker?"

"Something like that."

"Why would she let me see it, and not Cla—not the woman I was with yesterday?"

Florina shook her head. "I don't know."

"Did children die in this place?"

Florina shifted on her seat, pointing her knees away from her. She plucked at a loose thread on her apron. "I don't know," she mumbled.

"You know something."

Florina started crying. She spoke without turning her head, as though she were pleading with the door. "Where is Doreen?" she said. "Why hasn't she come back to see me?"

"How can Doreen have this power, Florina?" Regina said. "Who—" "What—is she?"

"Please leave," Florina said, placing her hands over her ears. "Please."

Regina stumbled out into the sunlight and hailed a tricycle. There was one final person to visit. Loretta Juni's house in San Jose stood away from the road, behind a patch of land with mango trees. Regina alighted in front of a sari-sari store that was already closing up, and asked the man behind the wire screen, just to make sure.

"Yes, that's Ma'am Lorie's place," he said, puffing on a cigarette sticking out of the corner of his mouth.

Ma'am Lorie. So, she was either a teacher or someone very rich.

She didn't seem *too* rich, basing solely on the house, but then her family probably also owned the lot with the mango trees in front, which was large enough to accommodate one or two more houses. The house had a porch, painted white, with a wooden table and a couple of chairs, perfect for entertaining visitors. There was a cardboard sign on an easel on the other side of the porch, the words written in beautiful script: *Free Art & Piano Lessons, Sat-Sun, 2 to 4 PM. By appointment. Inquire inside.* Below the words were watercolor sketches of a piano and an artist's palette. *Ah*, Regina thought. *So, a teacher then.*

Regina knocked on the door. She was assailed by the smell of turpentine when the door opened.

Loretta Juni appeared out of the heady haze, wearing dark purple eyeliner and red lipstick, her hair tied back with a silk scarf. There were spots of paint on her hands and upper arms, on her clavicle and her throat and on one cheek.

"Hello!" she said. "How can I help you?"

"Hi," Regina said. "Sorry to disturb you. I just want to ask you a couple of quick questions."

"Is this about a class?" Loretta said, and glanced at her sign on the easel. "Because I'm afraid I won't be having classes this weekend."

"No," Regina said. "It's not about your classes."

"In that case—" Loretta shrugged and turned on her heel, gesturing for her to enter. Regina followed her into a very large room filled with expensive furniture. To their right was the dining room, to their left the living room. Up ahead was a short flight of stairs leading to the rest of the house. Dotting the floor were vases and gold sculptures of women in long flowing dresses. They looked like award statuettes.

The living room—with the sala set pushed back against the wall and the floor covered with plastic and old newspapers—was currently serving as Loretta's workspace. Resting on a black easel was a four-foot-tall canvas. Loretta was working on a life-size, highly detailed painting of a girl, wearing a blue dress and black school shoes with lace socks. The girl's eyes were covered with a strip of black paint. In the white space around the girl were passages, snippets of redacted conversation.

Why did ████ take us away? You have no ██████████ Tell them that ██████████ and I ████████

"I'm starting a series called 'Anonymous,'" Loretta said.

"It—" *reminds me of Clara* "—is very compelling," Regina said.

"Thank you." Loretta smiled at her. "Let's sit over here. Would you like something to drink?"

Sitting by Loretta's dining room table with a glass of water, Regina asked the same questions. Do you know anyone named Emil Macaraeg? Or Diana de Leon? Or Doreen something? Would you know if there was a research facility built in this town?

"I haven't heard of it, if there was one." Loretta predictably replied no to every single question. Of course. Regina nodded to herself. She was just about to thank her and say goodbye when Loretta said, "Why don't you show me the map?"

Regina put down her glass of water and stared at her. Slowly, Loretta's expression went from amiable curiosity to terror-filled realization. The hand she had reached out to Regina curled and went back to her lap.

"I never told you about a map," Regina said.

"You mentioned it earlier," Loretta said, giggling. "Don't be silly." But her eyes belied her nervous *Oh shit* awareness. Regina knew and Loretta knew Regina knew and Regina knew that Loretta knew that Regina knew.

Regina stood up. "I'm sorry, but I have to go. Thanks for your time."

"Wait!"

She didn't run, just walked briskly. When she pulled the door open, her brother Luciano was standing on the porch.

"Kuya?" she said, surprised and confused. She saw him raise his arms and form an O with his mouth, but she was not able to hear what he was going to say. Something hard and fast hit the back of her head, and everything faded to black.

PART
II

Homecoming

CHAPTER 10

Luciano was a slow learner as a child. He took longer than most children to grasp instructions and understand what was asked of him, both on the farm and in school. This resulted in spankings and verbal abuse, shaming, and name-calling. *Tanga, bobo, mangmang.* He got held back in first grade because he couldn't finish his final exam, telling the teacher that he didn't know how to answer any of the questions. Luciano, who created stories by drawing stick figures on the mud outside their farm, was a proud child, a child weary of his position in the hierarchy of the world. He responded to taunting from his classmates with his fists. He was branded a "problem child."

When he turned 10, his parents had Regina, and they left him alone to his own devices.

Luciano, now 29, did research for the government and some private entities on agricultural concerns. How to better irrigate farmlands, how to make *palay* more resistant to pests. Luciano made good money doing consultancy work—there were, apparently, not a lot of serious Agriculture majors walking around—and last year helped write a research paper that he and a team presented in a conference in Kuala Lumpur. In the mornings, during weekends and when he was not busy, he would stroll around UP Los Baños, where he felt the air was sweeter and the trees livelier than in the university's flagship campus in Diliman. He would sit under a tree and rest his back against its bark. He loved his life, but every day he knew he was living on borrowed time, and what he was doing was penance. It was absolutely necessary for him that he did something worthwhile with this life.

Back in Heridos, Dr. Emil Macaraeg was shaking a patient's hand, telling her to take a seat for a minute while he made a call. He had to make an *urgent* call, but Luciano's sister Regina wanted to ask one final question. Emil felt blood rush to his head when she mentioned "research facility"—*Say, a facility for researching genetics?*—and he said something flippant and hopefully funny. He saw Regina laugh, but couldn't absorb what she said next. It didn't matter because she was turning away now. Emil entered his clinic, locked the door, and fished his cell phone out of his coat pocket.

Luciano was on one of his morning strolls. He was sitting on the forest floor, enjoying the sunlight streaming through the branches of the trees, when his ringing cell phone broke the calm.

He sighed. He should have just left the damn thing in the apartment.

"Em," he said, pouring his disappointment into that single syllable. *This better be important.*

"Where are you?"

Luciano picked out a leaf from his hair. "Work."

"You better drive home right now."

Emil sounded panicky. He never panicked.

"What's going on, Em?"

"Your sister just came from my clinic."

"Why? Is she sick?"

"Did you know that she worked with *Doreen* in an office?"

"Doreen?" He had not spoken to Doreen in a long while. He was on his feet now, pacing, the moment of meditation forgotten. "She never mentioned that to me."

"Doreen used an alias. Diana de Leon."

Luciano stopped walking. "I've heard that name," he said. *Think.* "She told me that name. Last night. She asked if I knew anyone named Diana. What is going on, Em?"

"Doreen left her something. A map."

"A map?"

"On the other side of the page she wrote my name and Lorie's."

"What?"

"And right now, just before she left, Regina asked me about if I knew anything about a facility conducting research on genetics."

Luciano felt a throbbing in his temples, what his colleagues called a "stress headache", as though it were too good and too noble to be a run-of-the-mill headache and so deserved a qualifier. "How did she—"

"The map, Luke," Emil said. "How could she possibly know about the center? The map led her to it. Doreen led her to it."

"Why would Doreen do this?"

"I don't know," Emil said. "Regina said their office couldn't contact her. I'll try calling the last number she left me, but I doubt I'd be able to reach her."

"I don't understand."

They fell silent. In Heridos, Emil sank in his chair, closing his eyes. In Los Baños, Luciano walked out of the shade into the sunlight.

Emil broke the silence. "Doreen has always been—"

"What?"

Emil sighed. "She was never completely on-board, Luke."

"Well, we all feel guilty, don't we? It's not like she's the only one hurting." Luciano took a deep breath. The anger felt like a physical weight, weighing him down.

"Do you remember the map?" Luciano said.

"Yes. We need to get to Ka Edgar's property. Are you coming home?"

Luciano exhaled, slowly. "I'm on my way."

"Take care of yourself," Emil said. "Meet me here first. I'll call Lorie."

Luciano threw some clothes and his wallet into the back-seat and drove out of the parking lot of his apartment building. Regina was not answering her phone. Later, while he was stuck in traffic on SLEX, he received a text from Emil saying that Regina had not yet visited Lorie. This was either a good thing or a bad thing, the bad thing being Regina already had all the answers she needed and had no more need to interrogate Lorie. The good thing being he could still intercept. And do what? Luciano's head throbbed. He'd figure it out with Emil. Right now, he had to focus on his driving and—

His phone danced on the dashboard. Regina. He hit Speaker and tried to calm himself. Tried to sound carefree and casual. "Oh, hey Reg," he said, and instantly winced. *Oh, hey Reg? What the hell?*

"You called me three times."

He didn't know if it was just his paranoia, but to him Regina sounded suspicious.

"I just wanted to check up on you." He smiled even if he didn't feel like it, just so his voice would sound believably cheerful. "Did you go out?"

"Just to the computer shop."

He didn't believe her, but this was not the time to push it.

"Oh, okay. How are the parents?"

"They're okay. What's going on?"

Oh no. "What do you mean?" Oh no. Oh no.

"Why are you checking up on me? You're not dying, are you?" Pause. "Are you driving?"

"No," he said, and lifted the phone off the dashboard. "I'm at my apartment. Why would I be driving?" He laughed, a forced *eh he he he.*

"You're weird."

"*You're* weird."

"I have a question."

"Mm."

"Does the name Maximillian Fortes mean anything to you?"

Luciano felt like he was falling. She *had* seen the place. She wouldn't have known that name if she hadn't— "Sounds like a Bond villain."

"He does, doesn't he. Do you know anyone named—Never mind."

"What?"

"It's nothing. Look, I'll take a nap."

"Okay," Luciano said. "Bye-bye." He dropped the phone on the dashboard and hit his palms on the steering wheel. "Fuck!" he said. "Fuck, fuck, *fuck.*"

He felt a breeze on the back of his neck, and all of a sudden, the car was filled with the smell of flowers—strong and insistent, like the scent of ylang-ylang—and wet earth. It was the smell of a garden after a strong rain. Luciano groaned. Today of all days.

"Oh, come *on.*"

"Is that the way to greet an old friend?" There was a man now sitting on the passenger seat, and a woman smiling from the backseat. Spirits and gods used to roam the town of Heridos, but even outside Heridos they appeared to Luciano, checking in on him, saying hi. Especially these two, who were probably the most stubborn gods Luciano had the good (and bad) fortune to meet.

He took a deep breath (*just get it over with*) and smiled. "Greetings, Mapulon," he said to the God of Seasons now busy buckling his seatbelt, and "Greetings, Amihan," he said to the North Wind in the backseat.

"Greetings," Amihan said with a smile. Wind played with the curled ends of her black hair and circulated in the car. Luciano switched off the air-conditioning.

"Was that so hard?" Mapulon said, and patted his arm. Luciano's arm felt warm where Mapulon touched him.

"You look like you just came from a wedding," Luciano said.

"How lovely, Mapulon," Amihan said, smoothing down her white dress. "He comments on our finery."

"This is great," Luciano said, "but I would rather be alone right now."

"I see you're heading back to Heridos," Mapulon said, as though he didn't hear. "It's been a while."

"Any reason for this sudden homecoming?" Amihan said.

"Nothing, really," Luciano said, feigning nonchalance. "I just wanted to see my sister."

Luciano saw Amihan glance at the rear-view mirror, but she wasn't looking at him. She had locked eyes with Mapulon. Luciano sighed.

"Listen," Mapulon said, "if you need any help—"

Can you turn back time? "You can't help me," he said.

"I'm sure our assistance—"

"Just get out of my car," Luciano said. "Please."

The smell of ylang-ylang slowly dissipated and was replaced by an electric smell, a faint burning, a herald of a storm.

"Where is Dumangan?" Mapulon asked.

Luciano kept his eyes on the road. Like a cop without an arrest warrant, Mapulon couldn't keep him in this interrogation room of his, couldn't compel him to answer.

"Not now," Amihan said, and the God of Seasons turned away.

"Just call us," Mapulon said, his voice low, as if he were gritting his teeth, "if you need our help."

Luciano turned the air-con back on and drove, alone, to Heridos.

CHAPTER 11

It was nearly 4 PM when Luciano reached the Poblacion. He parked on the side of the road near the hospital, and spotted Emil waiting outside, under a Duhat tree. He was not wearing his white doctor's coat, but he was carrying his black messenger bag, which Luciano knew doubled as a first-aid kit. He had his hands in his pockets and was staring off into the distance with a grim expression on his face. He relaxed into a small smile when he saw Luciano approach, his shoes kicking up dust.

"Well," Emil said.

"Well," Luciano said. "Here I am." He stood with his feet apart and his arms akimbo, as though bracing himself for an embrace, or a punch in the gut.

Emil gave him neither. "It's good to see you," he said, standing at a distance. "It's been a long time."

"I know," Luciano said. "How are you, though? Are you still having those episodes? Have you been taking your medicine?"

Emil was a sickly child. From a very young age he suffered from blinding headaches, followed by staring spells that adults mistook for inattention and mental retardation. He was having small epileptic seizures four to five times a week. But this was not the sort of seizure that his parents knew. It came without the mouth frothing and the limb flailing; without the drama they often saw on TV shows. So, they thought he was just slow. When he turned eight, he had *that* kind of seizure—*grand mal*—during a big family dinner, scaring his relatives, leaving them thinking that he had been possessed.

Emil was staring at the branches of the Duhat tree.

"Em?" Luciano said in alarm, thinking he was having one of his spells right now. "Are you all right? Can you hear me?"

"Calm down," Emil said. "Look."

Luciano looked up. Perched on a high branch was a figure with deep purple eyes and coal-black skin. It resembled a small child with elongated limbs. It stretched its legs and sat on the branch as if it were a swing, and looked at them. The look was not malicious, just curious.

"Hello there, little spirit," Emil said.

Luciano couldn't see the spirit's mouth, but they heard its voice just fine. "You can see me?"

"Clearly."

"How is that possible?"

"It's a long story," Luciano said. He lowered his head a little to make it look like he was just talking to Emil. There were still people milling about, and he didn't want to attract attention.

"I heard you talking about a girl," the spirit said, moving down the tree. Emil and Luciano stepped back so they could see it without craning their necks. "Someone named Regina."

"I spoke to Lorie on the phone," Emil explained. To the Duhat spirit he said, "That's correct. Do you have information about Regina?"

"A girl named Regina was here earlier," the spirit said. "Before noon."

"Really?" Luciano said. "What was she doing here?"

"Waiting," it replied. "Another girl approached her. She called herself Clara."

"Who the hell is Clara?" Luciano said.

Emil shrugged. "I have a patient named Clara," he said. "What did they talk about?" Emil asked the spirit.

"Another name," it said. "Maximillian Fortes."

Luciano and Emil exchanged a look.

"*Clara* said this name?" Emil said.

"Regina did. Clara recognized it. It moved her to tears."

"Who is this Clara?" Luciano whispered to Emil.

"Is this helpful?" the spirit said.

"Yes," said Emil, and patted his pants pockets, his messenger bag, and the pocket on his shirt. "I haven't done this in a while. I'm afraid I have nothing to offer you, except my thanks."

"Well," the spirit said, crawling back up the tree, back to where the leaves were thick. "Someone should harvest the fruit of this tree. Such a shame to let good fruit paint the ground."

Emil glanced at the stains on the pavement. "Of course," he said. "You're right. I will have this done."

"Thank you." The spirit gave them a little bow, turned to reach for another branch, and disappeared from view.

"Hello?" someone standing behind them said.

Loretta stood squinting and sweating under a big black umbrella. She was wearing a pair of glasses with red plastic frames, and there were swatches of dried blue paint on her hands and elbows. She scratched the flaking surfaces on her skin as she tried to make out who they were.

"Look at you!" Emil said, smiling at her. "Little Lorie."

"What's this about Regina?" she said without returning the smile. "Sorry I'm chipping off paint. I left in a hurry. I'm joining this group exhibit in Baguio and I'm still three or four paintings behind."

Luciano didn't know Loretta had started wearing glasses. He didn't know she had moved on from making watercolor sketches to working with oil paint on canvases. He didn't know she was joining an exhibit. They updated each other whenever they changed cell phone numbers, but that was the extent of their sense of loyalty.

Luciano had once hoped to never see them again.

"We'll tell you on the way," Luciano said. "Come on."

"But," Loretta said, running after them, her umbrella bobbing up and down, "where are we going?"

"The old man's farm," Luciano said.

Loretta responded to the update with a shrill "Why the hell didn't you tell me sooner?" which rebounded inside the car like an echo.

Emil sighed. "Precisely because of *this*. You'll start shouting at the top of your lungs."

"What was Doreen *thinking?*" Loretta said. She turned to Luciano. "Has your sister spoken to you yet?"

"The last time I spoke to her was on my way here," he said. He didn't tell them about his unexpected passengers.

"Ah, shit," Loretta said. She sat back, massaging the bridge of her nose.

"It will be fine," Luciano said.

"How can you say that?" she said, screaming again, and Emil winced. "What will you say if Regina starts asking you questions?"

"Nothing," he replied.

"Oh, good, and let her believe she is losing her mind."

"Lorie, give it a rest," Emil said. "Have you been skipping your medication again?"

Luciano glanced quickly at Emil, who looked as shocked as he was.

"How dare you," Loretta said. "How dare you ask me that. You're just as bad as them."

"I'm sorry," Emil said.

"This has nothing to do with my mood!" Loretta said. "We have a legitimate reason to panic!"

"Will everyone," Luciano said, "just calm down?" They were approaching the property. Luciano could drive right up to the farm, but that would mean leaving his car parked out in the open, under the sun. He slowed down and stopped under a clump of trees on the side of the road.

They got out to reach the property on foot. Emil, the only person in the group who had seen the map, led the way. They walked without speaking. Luciano glanced toward the farm and felt, one after the other: anger, shame, pity, loneliness. Luciano felt Loretta sidle up to him and offer to share her umbrella.

"Thank you," he said.

"I'm sorry about earlier," Loretta said. Luciano sighed and placed his arm around her. There was a time, so long ago, when they were close.

"I can't believe we're back here," Loretta said.

They reached the trees. Emil stood staring at a spot for a minute, walked one way, stopped, and walked to the other.

"What's going on?" Luciano asked.

"It's not here," Emil said. "The entrance. It's supposed to be here."

"Maybe we're in the wrong spot," Luciano said, and walked the way Emil had gone, looking through the trees again, as though a path was something a person could easily miss.

"Luke," Emil said. "Stop."

Luciano, busy looking for a pathway, was only half-listening. "What?"

"Stop," Emil repeated. Loretta stood beside him, fidgeting with the handle of her umbrella, looking like she was embarrassed for them all.

"We don't have permission," Loretta said. "Remember? We told Doreen to keep it from everyone, even from us."

Luciano stopped walking and looked up.

"It's all right," Loretta said. "We've all forgotten. It was a long time ago."

But Luciano once again was only half-listening. He had glanced, past Emil's shoulder, at a tricycle stop on the side of the road.

"What is it?" Emil and Loretta glanced back, squinting.

Luciano said, "Oh no."

He dragged them deeper into the woods, down to a spot where the trees were so thick the leaves blocked out the sun. On a friendlier day it would have led them to a clearing, a sidewalk, a quadrangle, but it was not a friendly day. It was a truly shitty, horrendous day, as far as Luciano was concerned, so it only led them to more trees.

Emil brushed leaves off his pants legs. "Maybe we should just head back to the—"

"Shh!"

They could only see two vague shadows through the trees, but the voices carried. The first voice Luciano heard was unfamiliar, but the voice that replied was definitely Regina's.

"It's not here. Nothing's here. I don't—"

"Clara? Breathe. Relax."

Luciano looked toward Emil. *Clara?*

"Son of a bitch! Clara, listen. I really—" Something unintelligible. "—make it up. There was a clearing right here just this morning!"

They continued to speak but Luciano couldn't hear them anymore.

It seemed to take the girls forever to leave. When the shadows disappeared, they waited for five more minutes—Luciano staying his companions with a hand in the air, *wait*—before he said, "*Now* we head back to the car."

It was possible that Regina and Clara were just heading home, but Luciano couldn't risk it. Maybe they were heading somewhere to talk about it. Maybe they could lead them to Doreen.

"It sounded like Clara," Emil said, panting a little as they hoofed it back to the car.

"What?"

"It sounded like my patient."

They got into the car and slammed the doors. "Damn it," Luciano said, changing gears. "What is going on?"

"She saw it," Loretta said. Luciano drove. The light was starting to fade. He knew what "it" referred to but he was too confused to focus on it.

There were only two vehicles on the road—the tricycle the girls took, and his car. He kept his distance, hoping he was far away enough for Regina to fail to read his plate number.

When darkness fell, the last of the sunrays glittering and winking out between gray clouds, Luciano saw something break away from one of the trees and fall on the back of the tricycle. It was thin and flimsy, like a veil, or a spider's web. Dark like the underside of storm clouds.

He was hoping his eyes were just deceiving him, he was just tired, he needed to sleep, but, "Did you see that?" Loretta said. "Did anybody else see that?"

"Luke," Emil said.

"What are we going to do?" Loretta said. "What are we going to do?"

What else could Luciano do? Ram the tricycle from behind? He felt fear grip his insides like a vise.

"Luke," Emil said again. "We need to do something."

What?

Luciano said two names, and felt Emil and Loretta instantly pull away, as though he had set himself on fire. Then Loretta was screaming, because the smell of flowers had blossomed inside the car, and sitting on either side of her in the backseat were Amihan and Mapulon.

"Well," Mapulon said, "that took you long enough."

"Can you help me?" Luciano said, and he saw Amihan raise a finger.

The dark veil tore itself off the tricycle and hung, suspended, in midair. Luciano stopped the car. The tricycle sped away as if nothing had happened, and nothing did.

Night had fallen, and their only source of light was the car's headlights. Within the twin beams they watched the veil twirling like a dust mote. It was the size of a small tablecloth.

They all alighted. Mapulon stood directly beneath the spirit and lifted his hand. It swooped down, like nail filings to a magnet, and turned into a struggling, bat-like figure. Mapulon had his arm around its neck.

"There we are," he said. "Why don't you tell us what this is all about?"

The dusk spirit kicked and clawed at his hand. "How dare you lay hands upon me?" it said in a deep voice. "Filthy mortal! Disgusting meat-shell! What potion gave you this strength? What prayer? You mortals and your stupid rituals! The Mistress shall hear about this!"

Amihan giggled, and her subdued laughter sounded like a tinkling bell. The spirit stopped moving and looked at her.

"Filthy mortal?" Mapulon said. A strong wind blew, parting the clouds, and the moon shone. "Disgusting meat-shell?" There was enough light for Luciano to see that Mapulon was not smiling anymore. The God of Seasons released the dusk spirit, settling him on the ground, and the spirit didn't move an inch.

"Oh," it said. "Oh, no."

The moon disappeared behind clouds again.

"My Lord," it said, bringing its hands together in a gesture of supplication. "My Lord, forgive me, this useless one did not recognize you." It turned to Amihan. "My Lady—"

"You don't look at her," Mapulon said, an edge to his voice. "You don't address her. She is older than us. Older than the sky. Older than these fields."

"Oh, it's all right," Amihan said with a scoff. The dusk spirit lowered its head. Luciano felt almost sorry for it.

"Now," Mapulon said, "tell us who sent you."

"I came of my own volition, my Lord."

"Then for whom are you doing this?"

"Hukluban," the dusk spirit said.

Mapulon didn't react at once, which to Luciano felt even worse. The God of Seasons stood on the side of the road with his hand on his hips, his face turned away. *Take a deep breath. Count to ten.* It was like watching a volcano try hard not to explode. Amihan did not move at all, not even to glance at them.

"And what did the Goddess of Death want with those girls?" Mapulon asked.

"We have heard—" The dusk spirit was quaking under his gaze "—we have heard long ago she was promised 30 souls, and she only had 29."

Luciano felt a jolt.

"One soul escaped. I am on my way to capture it to curry favor with the Mistress, even though the other night spirits say the soul is protected." The spirit looked up for a quick glance and looked down again. "Only now do I understand the level of her protection."

No one corrected the spirit's wrong impression.

"How long ago since this soul escaped?" Mapulon asked.

"Many mortal years ago."

He nodded. "You may go now," he said. "And breathe no word of this to anyone else."

The dusk spirit looked up, its eyes wide, perhaps surprised the god was letting him leave, just like that. "Thank you," it said. "Thank you for mercy." It stood up and flew away, turning into a mass of gray dust.

Luciano felt a hand cling to the back of his shirt. Loretta's.

"Hukluban?" Mapulon said, turning to them, and Luciano felt his eyes sting, as though he were facing the sun. Behind him, Loretta whimpered and twisted his shirt. "Hukluban is involved?"

They said nothing.

"What have you done?" Mapulon said.

Amihan moved forward and reached for him. "Come now," she said. "Let us leave the children."

"Sooner or later you will have to tell us," Mapulon said, and together the two gods walked away from the headlights and into the darkness.

Loretta was crying.

"Someone escaped?" Luciano said. The three of them stood in front of the car. Emil was standing with his back to the light, and Luciano couldn't see his face. "We need to know more about this patient of yours, Em."

"I'm tired," Loretta said, sniveling. "I'm so tired."

"We'll have to go home now, Luke," Emil said.

Luciano took a deep breath. "I can't go home. I can't face Regina. Not now."

"Then stay at my place for a little while," Emil said. "Come on. It's dark. We need to get out of here."

Loretta sobbed all throughout the ride back to her house. She didn't reply when Emil offered to stay with her that night. She didn't reply when Luciano touched her hair and told her to take of herself.

Emil lived in a two-bedroom house just a short walk from the hospital. The gate was only large enough to accommodate one person at a time. Emil had pots upon pots of wilting flowers and herbs on his front porch. The smell of sage and mint was strong and calming.

"I got those plants from Guiguinto," Emil said, when he saw Luciano looking at his lifeless garden. "They're planted on soil that did not come from here. And yet—" He shrugged.

"There are still trees around," Luciano said.

"Yes, but they look dull," Emil said. "Haven't you noticed? Like they're already dying."

He took out his keys. "Is this house yours or your parents'?" Luciano asked as Emil looked for the right key.

"Mine," he said. "I bought it."

"You bought your own house?"

"I got it for cheap. They're practically giving away the houses on this road."

Emil opened the door and dropped his bag on the sofa. Luciano sat down beside the bag with a sigh, his clothes on his lap. Emil returned with a cold bottle of beer and sat down beside him.

Luciano took a swig and coughed. The beer burned. He couldn't remember the last time he drank.

"Are you all right?" Emil asked.

No one's all right, Luciano very nearly said.

"We need to find Doreen," he said instead.

Emil sat back on the sofa, his head on the backrest, and closed his eyes. He remained like this until Luciano finished his beer.

"Maybe she got tired of living like this," Luciano said, placing the bottle on the floor. He sat back, mimicking Emil's pose.

"Living like this?" Emil said.

"Isn't this punishment already?"

Emil was silent for a moment.

"What would happen if someone cut down that Duhat tree?" he said, and Luciano opened his eyes. He saw Emil looking at him.

"What do you mean?"

"The Duhat spirit will disappear," Emil said, replying to his own question. "It is a sentient manifestation of nature— sentient, but just a manifestation. It will disappear, without a peep, without protest. What it will experience is not death. When a soap bubble bursts, you don't say 'The bubble died.' Someone cuts down the Duhat tree, and there will be no retribution."

"Unless you kill a god," Luciano said, because wasn't that what Emil wanted to hear?

"Living like this," Emil said, "this is not punishment, Luke. Punishment is exile. Punishment is every single spirit and god knowing what we did. Punishment is that Duhat spirit spitting on our faces instead of talking to us."

"Em—"

"Punishment is Regina knowing," Emil said. "Do you want her to know?"

"No," Luciano said, rattled. "Of course, not."

"Punishment is not something you impose on yourself," Emil said. "You can fool yourself and say you're already paying for what we did, but the truth is we're living good lives, all five of us."

"Even Florina?"

Emil lifted his bag off the floor. "You can take my room, the guest room doesn't have a mattress," he said, and left him there.

CHAPTER 12

"So, what's up?" Loretta said. They were inside her house, Luciano sitting cross-legged on the floor, Emil standing behind her with his arms crossed, watching her add white paint to the little girl's blue dress on the canvas.

Luciano felt like he was three seconds away from falling asleep, either from the turpentine or from being mesmerized by Loretta's small brushstrokes. "What do you mean?" he asked.

Loretta replied without turning away from her canvas. "You look like you just had a big fight."

Luciano stiffened and Emil cleared his throat. It was late afternoon, after Emil's clinic hours. Luciano left his house early in the morning and they arrived at Loretta's separately. They had not spoken since the night before.

"That's a nice painting," Emil said. "I don't think you've ever painted canvas that large. Is it going to be a part of a series?"

"It's a self-portrait," Loretta said, and painted an angry black swatch over the girl's eyes.

"Oh," Luciano said, surprised and saddened.

There were words around the girl.

Why did they take us away?
You have no right.

Tell them that I am lost and I need saving.

Loretta started painting over some of the words with black paint.

Emil cleared his throat again.

"I don't have any information about Clara," he said, "save for her health records."

"Did she need surgery?" Loretta asked.

"No, just medicine for arrhythmia. She's also taking medication for anxiety."

"Zoloft?" Loretta asked, glancing over a shoulder. "Anafranil?"

Loretta as a child had extreme panic attacks, leaving her a trembling, choking, incoherent mess in the middle of class, or while lining up at the school cafeteria. The attacks started when she was six, after she saw a playmate get crushed by a speeding truck. Before long, panic attacks preceded the arrival of her school bus, and she got left behind in her studies, a scenario that, for her high-achieving parents, simply would not do.

"She doesn't worry me," she said, turning back to her work. "That girl doesn't remember anything, and if she does, she won't be asking questions."

"Then why did she approach Regina about it?" Luciano said. "I saw them get on a jeep. I thought they were heading here, but—" He lifted his hands in exasperation and slapped his knees. "Now I don't know where they are."

"You should have followed them."

"I know." But Luciano reacted too late, and he was afraid of what he would find. "They might head here next, so keep them here and try to get as much information from them as you can."

Loretta kept on painting. She didn't reply for so long that Luciano thought she didn't hear.

"How old are you, Em?" she said.

"*What?*" Luciano said.

"What?" Emil said.

"How old are you?" Loretta repeated. "Based on your birth certificate."

Emil sighed and sat on the floor. "I'm thirty-three."

"And you're still alone?"

"*You're* still alone."

"But you're thirty-three. Luke and I, we're not even thirty yet."

"So there's a deadline for these things?" But Emil was smiling, relaxing. Loretta had panic attacks, but she was the only one who could calm them down like this.

Emil said, "There was a girl once."

A pause. Loretta and Luciano turned their heads to look at him, like sunflowers tracking the sun.

"And?" Loretta said.

"She was a nurse at the hospital," Emil said, who was looking elsewhere. "We lived together for a while, but it didn't last long. She found a job in Oman. They'll pay her four times what she's making here, so it's really a no-brainer."

"She *lived* with you?" Loretta said, whose comprehension snagged and stayed on this single detail. "How come this is the first time I'm hearing about this?"

Emil shrugged.

"If not for the job abroad," she said, "would she have stayed with you?"

Emil shook his head. "It wouldn't have lasted, either way," he said.

Loretta picked up her brush again, focusing on the girl's hemline. "I can't imagine myself growing old with anyone but you guys," she said. "Unless I can commit myself to lying every single day. I bet that's what got to you, huh, Em? I bet that was it. I get confused. Just a while ago I called this my *self*-portrait." She wiped her face, leaving a blue streak on one cheek. "I can't even get the story straight."

There was a knock on the door.

"Oh," Loretta said, as Luciano and Emil leapt to their feet. "Do you think that's them?"

"Remember, just act natural," Luciano said, and headed with Emil up the stairs to the kitchen. "And try to find out as much as you can."

"Act *natural*, Lorie," Emil said.

"Stop saying that!" Loretta said. "You're making me nervous!"

"It's all right," Emil said. "Calm down."

Loretta waited for them to disappear down the hallway, and walked to get the door. There was only one girl standing on the porch. Regina. Where's the other one? she nearly asked, and bit her tongue.

"Hello!" Loretta said, and winced inwardly at her forced cheeriness. "How can I help you?"

"Hi. Sorry to disturb you. I just want to ask you a couple of quick questions."

Okay. Okay.

"Is this about a class?" she said, and congratulated herself for her apparent nonchalance. She leaned forward to glance at the sign advertising her classes. Act natural. "Because I'm afraid I won't be having classes this weekend."

"No. It's not about your classes."

"In that case—" Loretta shrugged and without glancing back, gestured for Regina to enter. She thought she was doing very well in the department of acting naturally. She saw Regina admiring the painting. "I'm starting a series called 'Anonymous,'" she said. They sat by the dining table. She offered the girl a drink. The questions came, one after the other. Act natural. Frown. Look perplexed.

In the kitchen, Luciano was feeling antsy. "I'll step out," he whispered to Emil, and opened the back door. Emil followed after a few seconds. They walked to the side of the house. The curtains were drawn, making it safe to pass.

"About last night—" Luciano began.

"It's all right," Emil said. "We're all jumping out of our skin."

Luciano didn't know what else to say after that. They stood by the windows, trying their best to hear.

Inside the house, Regina asked if Loretta knew of a research facility built in town, and "I haven't heard of it, if there was one," she said, after what she thought was a sufficient pregnant pause. Regina nodded to herself. Find out as much information as you can, and so Loretta said, "Why don't you show me the map?" and the very next second wondered, Wait, did Regina even mention the map?

Loretta watched her put down her glass of water, her face closing in. Regina now looked wary. Scared.

"I never told you about a map," Regina said.

Fuck. Loretta kept her smile on her face.

Fuck. Fuck this. Fuck my life.

"You mentioned it earlier," Loretta said, but even she didn't believe herself.

Regina stood up. "I'm sorry, but I have to go. Thanks for your time."

"Wait!"

That single word got through the windows. "What in the world," Luciano muttered, and moved to the door.

Regina walked quickly to the door, Loretta following on her heels. Loretta picked up one of the gold sculptures on the way. She wanted only one sculpture, but it was part of a set, so her parents just shipped everything home. In the place of one elegant dancer, Loretta received an army.

Regina pulled the door open. "Kuya?" she said.

Loretta held the sculpture by the legs and brought it down on the back of Regina's head. She felt the impact's vibration up her arms, the strange sensation waking her up.

"Oh no," she said. "Oh no." Oh no oh no oh no.

"Lorie!" Luciano rushed forward to hold Regina, who had crumpled to the floor. "What the *fuck*, Lorie, have you lost your mind?"

"What's going on?" Emil stepped up to the doorway and saw an unconscious Regina in Luciano's arm. "What happened?" he asked, and saw Loretta still clutching the gold sculpture.

"Is she dead?" Loretta said, shaking all over. "Did I kill her? Oh no."

"Move her forward," Emil said. "I need to close this door. You two are going to bring the entire neighborhood to this porch."

"Damn it!" Luciano told Loretta. "I told you to keep her here, not give her a concussion!"

"But she was running away!"

"Shut up," Emil said. "The both of you." He knelt in front of Luciano and touched the back of Regina's head, checked her eyes. Regina moaned softly.

"Reg?" Luciano said. But Regina was quiet again.

"She'll have a nasty bump," Emil said, "but she's fine."

"Are you sure? Lorie, I swear, if you—"

"Calm down. Can you carry her? Let's move her to the bedroom."

"I'm sorry," Loretta mewled, over and over, as Luciano picked up Regina and moved her deeper into the house. Loretta was still holding the sculpture in her arms. Between the pleading and the eyeliner-stained tears flowing down her face, Emil thought she looked like an award-winning actress suffering a nervous breakdown.

"It's okay," Emil said, taking the sculpture from her, which in her panic she had held on to with a vise-like grip. Emil pried off her fingers one by one. "She's fine. You just panicked. Sit down and I'll get you some water."

"What are we going to do?" Loretta asked Emil's back as he walked to the kitchen. "What are we going to do?" she asked as Luciano returned to the living room, his shirt crumpled and his hair in disarray.

"We need to find Doreen," he said. "She needs to make this right."

It was not a very good answer. As far as Loretta was concerned, Doreen was already a lost cause. So, there was no solution. So, there was no hope. She had been wishing for a morning where she could just wave a hand, banishing everything that had gone wrong, and sit in front of her canvas with only music humming in her head.

"Here you go, Lorie," Emil said, reaching for her hand and making her limp fingers wrap themselves around a cold glass of water. "Luke, where did you put Regina?"

Luciano looked about ready to claw his eyes out. "What?" he said, distracted.

"Regina. Where'd you put her?"

"She's in Lorie's room."

Emil paused. "Is that the one with the purple curtains?"

"Yes?" Luciano stood up, sensing that something was wrong. "Why?"

Emil was already running back to the hallway. "She's not there."

CHAPTER 13

Purple curtains. Interesting. The last time Regina saw purple curtains in a room was during a party at a colleague's house. His wife had just given birth to a baby girl, and he was hanging purple curtains in the nursery. It was to complement the lilac walls, the pink ceiling, the white crib.

"Too much?" he had asked then.

Regina had smiled and replied, "The room looks like a big cake", which was her way of saying, Yes, it's a bit much.

A breeze was coming from the open window, rippling the purple curtains. Purple waves. Her Kuya Luciano. Luke. Didn't she just see him outside the door? The back of Regina's head throbbed. She was lying on her side on a soft, unfamiliar bed. What door, though, and where was she?

Wind blasted through the window. The purple curtains were now horizontal. When the curtains fell back against the frame, a man and a woman stood right in front of Regina.

She could see white cloth, brown skin, and long black hair. The woman approached the bed and bent over her. Regina was reminded of a day during her final year in college—a ten-hour thesis-writing marathon, followed by that moment when she opened the window and felt the cool breeze on her skin, the air smelling like the beginning of everything, and the end of everything.

Mmfff, Regina said, which at the moment was her way of saying, *Who are you and what the hell is going on here?*

The man had his back against the wall, one arm crossed over his chest, the other extended. He cupped his chin like a critic at an art gallery.

Art. Art gallery. Painting. Loretta Juni. Regina tried to stir but couldn't.

The man stepped forward and lowered his hands, placed them deep in his pockets. "What are we doing here?" He sounded exasperated. Regina was instantly frightened of him, whoever he was. He sounded like someone she wouldn't want to annoy.

"Hello," the woman said. Get me out of here, Regina tried to say, but she couldn't produce words, just noise.

"Isn't this what you'd call 'getting involved'?" said the man. "And besides, the girl knows nothing."

"Yes?" the woman said to Regina, and the man sighed loudly. "What is that?"

Get me out of here.

"Would you like to get out of here?"

Yes! Yes! Damn it, yes!

"Well, then." The woman turned into a bird so large she filled the entire room with her wings. She scooped up Regina and the man, and flew out of the window.

Loretta Juni gave me drugs, Regina thought, and was either struck blind or was pushed into a room so dark she couldn't see anything. She felt something solid against her back. She was lying on the ground.

"Now what?" the man said.

"Now," replied the woman, "we wait."

Regina woke up in the dark, on the side of the road, and started thinking of spirits, gods, and her grandmother.

La Reina Heridos. La Regina Heridos. The wounded queen. The wounded Regina.

And somehow Florina's house flew from the quadrangle and landed where she was. How convenient. *"What?"* Regina said after Florina opened the door. She looked past her and saw Diana or Doreen inside, her hip against the kitchen sink, pressing a bloody towel to her neck.

CHAPTER 14

"If this is just the tip of the iceberg," Clara said, "and this is what it's doing to me, then I'd rather it remained submerged, you know?"

She couldn't remember much of what happened after that. Everything that came after was a blur. The day inserted itself in bits and pieces. Sweat on her nape. Hair stuck in clumps to her forehead. Regina's hand on her arm. The roar of the tricycle. Dust in her eye. The smell of perfume, or the memory of it. *A classic scent that will never fade on your wrist. Beautiful notes of pink jasmine, iris, patchouli, amber, and vetiver. An unforgettable fragrance for an unforgettable—*

Clara sat on the edge of her bed, staring at the bottles of perfume, pills, hand cream, and lotion on her dresser. The house was empty and silent. Her parents were at the wet market, butchering pigs for sale. Later that week they would take the bus to Quezon City to visit her sister. Clara used to work full-time at a BPO in the same city, but one night she crossed the street, head filled with stress and antidepressants, and nearly got hit by a bus. She moved back to Heridos, back to her old room in her parents' house. She couldn't for the life of her find the willpower to butcher meat, so that was another failure. She wondered how she could fix herself. Meeting that doctor was a mistake. *Patchouli.* A big mistake. *Pink jasmine.*

Shut it down. Shut it all down.

Someone was knocking on the door. Not the front door, though. The back door.

"Who is it?" Clara asked, but opened the door just the same.

The first thing Clara noticed was the house with a brown door on their backyard, sitting there amidst the swaying shirts and dresses on the clothesline. There was a house on their backyard. *There was a house on their backyard.*

Clara turned to the person standing in front of her. The woman was about her height, and looked about her age. The woman looked familiar.

"Hi, Clara," she said.

Clara said nothing.

"You don't remember me," the woman went on. "But that's all right. We can try to start over." She offered her hand and smiled. "Hi. My name is Doreen."

Before Clara could say anything or understand what was happening, Doreen placed her arms around her and dragged her across the backyard into the house with the brown door.

Luciano, Emil, and Loretta ran out of the house to where the car was parked and climbed in. Luciano drove. Regina was injured. She couldn't have gone far.

They drove down the road with the abandoned school and houses until they saw a light through the thick branches of trees.

CHAPTER
15

"Who's with you?" Doreen said. "Amihan? Mapulon? Who's with you now?"

What? Regina walked into the house. She could hear someone crying.

"Diana?" Doreen? She wasn't sure what name to call her.

Doreen pressed the balled-up towel against her neck, looking like a shot putter. There were droplets of blood on her shirt. She was trying to look past Regina.

"Are they here now?" Doreen said, wide-eyed.

"What in the world are you talking about?" Regina said. Where have you been? What is going on? "What happened to your neck?"

Only then did she see Clara on the floor, hugging her knees behind one of Florina's shelves. The light thrown by the fluorescent in the living room threw shadows of the various knick-nacks onto Clara's face. She looked as if she were behind bars. Her right hand was bloody. There was a broken plate on the floor.

Regina called her name. Clara looked up and Regina saw how swollen and red her eyes were from crying.

"It's just a scratch," Doreen said, though the scratch continued to bleed when she removed the towel to check. "Damn it." She opened an overhead cupboard and pawed through its contents until a black zippered pouch fell on the counter.

"Give me some of that," Regina said, when Doreen pulled out a roll of gauze from the pouch. Regina squatted in front of Clara and took her bloodied hand.

Clara was shaking. Badly. "Get me out of here," she said in a tiny voice.

"It's okay," Regina said. "It's okay."

A car stopped outside. Regina peeked through a collection of plastic dinosaurs and saw Florina sitting on the sofa, her head turned toward the open door. What Regina saw next was an incredible thing, as incredible as seeing a house where it was not supposed to be: her brother walking through the door, followed by that doctor she had spoken to at the hospital—What was his name? Emil?—and Loretta Juni, who had the room with the purple curtains.

"Doreen!" her brother thundered. "Doreen, what are you—"

Regina stood up and stepped into the living room. "You better explain to me what's going on here."

She saw Luciano freeze. Loretta, who was running, crashed into him. Emil closed the door and leaned against it.

"Regina!" Luciano said. "I—Maybe we should all sit down and—"

"No!" she told her brother, and "Shut up!" she said to Emil, who was about to open his mouth. "I have had enough of this. Nobody speaks unless the first word that comes out of your mouth is an explanation."

"Regina—" Doreen said. There was now a square piece of gauze haphazardly taped on her neck.

"That better be the start of an explanation, Diana!" Regina said. "Or Doreen! Or whatever *the hell* your name is!"

"I'll explain."

It was Florina. She had her hand raised, like a child in class. Everyone, save for Regina and Clara, started speaking at the same time.

"Florina—"

"What do you mean—"

"What can you possibly—"

"You don't know anything," Luciano said.

"I know everything!" Florina screamed, the veins on her neck and forehead standing out like vines. "I remember everything!"

Doreen turned away and covered her face with her hands. Luciano placed a hand on Florina's shoulder.

"You can't be serious," he said. "Tell me you're lying."

Florina brushed off his hand.

Regina sat beside Florina. "Talk to me," Regina said, and was surprised to feel the burn of tears in the corner of her eyes. "Please. I feel like I'm losing my mind."

"I think I've lost my mind a long time ago," Florina said, and took her hands.

"No!" Luciano said. He tried to pull Regina away. "Stop it!"

"She deserves to know!" Doreen said. "She and Clara—look at Clara. We thought erasing her memory would help her, but we ruined her, Luke. We ruined everyone. When I walked into that office and saw Regina—when I heard her talking to other people about you Luke, about how *nice* you are—we can't go on living like this. This is not right."

But Regina could no longer hear them. All she could hear was Florina.

PART III

Daughter of Harvest

CHAPTER 16

Regina?

Can you hear me?

The first thing you need to understand is: we are not who we say we are.

We are the children of the harvest of Heridos. Our constant companions are Mapulon, the God of Seasons, and Dumangan, the God of Good Harvest.

We venerate Amihan, the North Wind, who helped create the land. The Mother of us all.

We are: Hamog, Sibol, Lupa, Ulap, Hangin. We are the spirits of dew and seedlings, of soil and clouds and rain. We are little spirits, nothing more, nothing less. We are inconsequential.

We are. *Were.* We were. We *were* spirits.

We are all still inconsequential.

I'm sorry. Let me start from the beginning. Or, at least, the beginning that makes sense.

Not very long ago, the town of Heridos consisted largely of farmlands and a few wooden houses that stood far apart from one another. In 1499, it was a vast nameless field occupied by tillers. In 1588, it became the site of the beheading of Esteban

Taes, who, along with several Tagalog and Kapampangan leaders, conspired to overthrow the Spanish colonizers. They called
it the Tondo Conspiracy, which lasted a measly year. The conspiracy was led by Agustin de Legazpi. Agustin also asked help
from the Japanese, who, as we all know, firebombed the Philippines years later, but that's 355 years later so we can't really
blame Agustin for trusting them.

The conspirators were exposed by a turncoat. While the
properties of some of the leaders were seized, plowed, and
sown with salt to keep the lands barren, the Spanish invaded
the town where Taes spilled his blood and gave it to *insulares*
whose *indios* tilled the land.

Estaba herido de muerte, the Spanish soldiers kept saying,
referring to Taes. He was mortally wounded. Later, the insulares baptized the town "Herido," which gossip mutated to
"Heridos."

Maybe those soldiers were trying to be funny.

I know, I know. I went too far back. But I just want to say:
go back far enough and you'll realize that every piece of land
you'll find yourself standing on has been claimed and lost and
re-claimed thousands of times. All land has witnessed its share
of sadness and tragedy. Every single piece.

I don't know. I feel like I just had to say that.

The largest of Heridos's farmlands belonged to the Cajucom family, who struck a deal with the local and national government in the 60's. The government bought a portion of their
land, and soon, construction began on that property. It was a
group of buildings, hidden from view by thick clumps of trees.
At the time, Heridos was the home of fewer than 5,000 peo-

ple. Many wondered why a government agency would decide to build a facility there, in the middle of nowhere.

Was it a school? A hotel? A hospital? A marketplace? People speculated, and in the end, it turned out to be all of the above.

A community began to grow around the Maximillian Fortes Center for Heredity & Genetics even before it formally opened. Scientists and researchers from the Institute would need a place to stay in the small town of Heridos. A place to eat. A place to raise their families. So the Institute hired workers from Heridos and neighboring towns. They began construction of a subdivision for the Center employees. Houses. Restaurants. A school. A place of worship.

Before long, researchers from the Center went around Heridos knocking on doors and approaching residents. The researchers—young, pleasant, and looking undoubtedly like out-of-towners with their jeans and rubber shoes and brightly colored shirts—said they were conducting "an unofficial census." *How many people live in this house? How many are earners, and how many are the dependents? If you are a parent, do you find raising your child/children challenging?*

It was a "neutral" question, but when residents ask "What do you mean by challenging?" the researchers say, "Do you think your child is problematic?"

Imagine for a moment that you are your own mother, Regina. You are thirty-two years old, married to a thirty-three-year-old. Ancient in that time and place. You are overwhelmed by your seven-year-old son who was not at all what you expected or what you dreamed your firstborn son to be. You dreamed of someone decisive, smart and quick, a miniature version of your husband, or your late father, a little boy who would say,

"I will take care of you, Mother!" But he just got held back in first grade at the elementary school. You just came back from a meeting with his teacher who said Luciano had punched a classmate. Again. "But he called me stupid!" your son said to you, and you wanted to say, *But you are! And now you have to be violent, too?*

Yes, you tell the pretty researcher named Florina, I think my son is problematic. And Florina smiles at you and writes something in her notebook.

The researchers return the year after, in 1976. You don't know what is happening inside the Center, but cars come and go and local businesses are flourishing. There are more restaurants now in the plaza, and researchers go crazy buying fresh produce at the market. They buy a lot and they don't haggle, which you like.

But you don't like them. Not at first, at least. You are fascinated by their city accent and their brightness, a little intimidated by their presence, but you are suspicious of them, and disdainful of the cheerful way they speak to you. Look at these children, you tell yourself, thinking they're better than me.

It is 1976. Proclamation 1081 is turning four years old. Your son is turning eight. He slaps your hand away whenever you reach for him, and you respond by slapping him in the face. Sometime in October of the present year, a national referendum will be called, and respondents will be asked to reply yes or no to two questions: *Do you want Martial Law to be continued?* and *Do you approve the following amendments to the Constitution?*

It is 1976, a bright Monday morning, and you are wondering how to respond to a different set of questions. Florina has entered your house with a *bilao* of Pancit Malabon and a fair-skinned woman wearing dark sunglasses. The woman's long hair is piled on top of her head in a bun, revealing tiny diamond studs on her earlobes. She removes her sunglasses and greets you a good morning. Florina is Flo to her colleagues, but with the residents she is Floring, a cute nickname. Dorothea Fortes could have been Doring, but she'll have none of that nonsense. She is Dr. Fortes or Doktora Thea or Doktora, and those are the names you call her.

In the living room, you and your husband sit on the sofa, while Dr. Fortes and Florina sit in armchairs. The Pancit Malabon and glasses of orange juice—sweating bullets, like you—sit on the coffee table. In the presence of Dr. Fortes's fair skin and diamond studs you feel a little diminished. You are suddenly ashamed of the rickety coffee table, of the horse tapestry hanging on the wall, and of your painting depicting cats and dogs playing a game of cards. The table still serves, horses mean good luck and pets playing poker is funny, but right now you are ashamed of all of them and you hate yourself for it.

"Where is Luciano?" Dr. Fortes asks with a smile that, to you, looks a bit predatory.

"He's in school," your husband replies.

"I see," the doctor says. "I hear he's been having problems in class?"

"Problems?" your husband says, and you nearly slap his hand for drawing it out. Just say it. Just say it and get it over it.

"Oh. Well. Yes. He is a bit slower than his classmates."

"I hear he's been getting into fights?"

"Where did you hear about this?" your husband says, defensive, and you see Florina glance at you.

From *me*. All right? They heard it from me.

"It's a small town, sir," Florina says. "And we're actually here to help."

"Help how?" he says. "He's slow. He won't be going to college. Nothing we can do about it."

Dr. Fortes pins him with a steady gaze, punctuates it with a dazzling smile. "No offense to the local elementary school," she says, "but the teachers there are not equipped to help your son. They are overworked and underpaid. There are too many students in each class. What Luciano requires is focused instruction that they cannot provide. He is just one boy, and there are hundreds of children to attend to." She turns to you. "We can provide this focus."

"We don't have money for this," your husband says, and the doctor shakes her head.

"The Center is open to children with such needs free of charge," she says. "All we require is your consent to let your child live on Center grounds, and your permission to allow us to use in our studies any data we gather during our interactions with your child."

"Free of charge?" Your husband is stuck on this detail. He cannot believe it.

That amorphous word—*interactions*—carries such weight. But you don't know this yet. And probably never will.

"And there are other children in the Center now?" you say, speaking for the first time.

"Yes, ma'am," Dr. Fortes says, and you are touched by the honorific. A doctor calling you ma'am. "A few from Heridos. Some from Malolos and Paombong, and even some from Manila."

"Children from Manila are coming here?"

"Yes. Some are already in high school, so, technically, these are no longer children, but teenagers." She leans forward, becomes conspiratorial. "We have taken in a disabled child, quite recently. A neighbor of yours. You might know the family."

"Ah," your husband says, and turns to you. "The Mongoloid next door."

"Ah," you say, and can't help but feel offended. "But my son is not—"

"We understand your concern," the doctor says. "These are all problematic cases, but each case is unique, and each case will be treated with the attention it requires."

"Who else are being admitted?" you ask.

"Epileptics," the doctor replies. "Children with attitude problems. Violent children. Handicapped children."

"But Luciano will be safe there?"

"Of course," the doctor says. "Florina here can show you a sample agreement. When would you like to have a tour of the Center?"

A comforting hand on a shoulder is an interaction. So is a conversation. So is a syringe containing a disease plunged into a vein, followed by a syringe containing the supposed cure. A new drug administered at 10 AM and again at 5:30 PM, every day for fourteen days, and the endless interviews that follow: *How did it make you feel?* Electrodes attached to temples. Bright lights flashing in a room to ensure sleep deprivation, and the endless interviews that follow. *How did it make you feel?*

You and your husband sign your name in behalf of your son, unwittingly saying yes to all these interactions, and more.

117

The parents who signed the agreement believe their children are hopeless cases. During those days it was not uncommon to hear stories of children being hit with sticks, locked in cages, and driven out of town and abandoned on the side of the road. They turn their children over to Dr. Fortes and the Center with gratitude, with relief, because, for once, they are allowed to believe that they are kind.

You believe you are kind. Even if you don't know exactly what it is they do inside the Center, even if you do not completely understand the agreement you just signed. You are kind because you are not proud. You are humble enough to say, *This is too much and I need your help.* You are hopeful your child will be fixed, and will be returned to you whole. Maybe then you can love him with the full vastness of your heart.

The agreement provides for a weekly visit, but the first meeting proves to be too difficult, too heartbreaking, your son hitting your thigh with tiny fists, screaming *You abandoned me! You abandoned me! You abandoned me!* Dr. Fortes tells you perhaps it is best if you don't see him for a while. You listen to the doctor. You stay away for a month. Living in a suddenly childless house, you and your husband rediscover a lost vigor. A lost affection.

This is also a sacrifice on your part, living without Luciano. But you are doing this for your child. You are being strong, for your child. This is for the best.

You say this to yourself, over and over, to silence the other voice that says: Luciano is not here, and I am happy.

CHAPTER 17

We were not concerned with any of this. Some of us, a small minority, were curious and fascinated, but most of us watched with detachment the rise of the Center's buildings and the corresponding movements of people and resources in and out of Heridos.

(Doreen of course would read up on it later, but that would be much later when the knowledge was useless and there was nothing we could do to change the situation.)

We traveled with Dumangan in those days. Every now and then he clothed himself in mortal flesh and walked among humans. There were many, many stories in Heridos about a young farmer no one had ever seen before suddenly showing up and working the fields from sunrise to sunset, an anonymous presence in a group of workers, every single one thinking he was the friend of the other. During lunch, he would sit cross-legged under the shade of a tree, eating his meal and not joining in the conversations, just listening and responding to the stories with a smile or a silent nod.

No one asked him questions. No one asked him who he was. Once (or so the stories went) a member of the Cajucom family thought he was moving too slowly and screamed at him on the field. That Cajucom was not able to get up from bed for three straight months, unable to eat rice or any other grain, or any animal that was fed grain, like chicken or pig or cow, and the man's family and farmers knew at once who exactly the man had offended.

Dumangan lived in a house that would appear in different locations every single day, as though it had legs. It was a one-story with a brown door and a rusty roof. The lights inside glowed yellow at night.

Yes, Regina. This was Dumangan's house.

Once a year, Dumangan would gather us to give us human bodies with which to experience the world for three days.

The first time he did this, Mapulon paid him a visit and said that what he was doing was dangerous.

"If you feel this perspective is necessary for them to learn," Mapulon said, "if you feel this is important, then I implore you not to assume a mortal body the same moment that they do. Do not make yourself as vulnerable as they are."

Dumangan only smiled and said Mapulon had so little faith in the people who had so much faith in him.

"And it is disappointing," Mapulon replied, "how much you underestimate them."

Clothed with a body, the first thing that hits you is *longing*. It hits you like a burn, like a deep pain between your eyes. And it is not just one longing. It is a chain of them, one after the other:

the longing for water

the longing for food

the longing to cover the hard, rough ground with something softer

the longing to cover the sun because it burns

the longing to get out of this, this existence we do not recognize

We *wanted* so much, and it was puzzling and painful. We couldn't articulate it. We did not know how or where to begin. We had never longed before.

We thought we were being punished and we just couldn't remember why.

It got worse before it got better. But it did get better. We learned when and how to respond to our hunger and our thirst. Before long, we even learned to enjoy the sun on our skin, even when it burns, and the wind on our face, even when it flattens the rice stalks. We learned to enjoy the gap in time between the want and its fulfillment. *I am tired now and I want to rest my legs, but later, later, there will be time to rest. Not now, but later, and it will be good, and this is all right. This is acceptable.*

We never got used to our bodies to the point that the perspective ceased to amaze us. The first time I fell on my hands and knees and scraped my skin, I was astonished by how easily I focused on this injury, how quickly the rest of the world fell away, and how effortlessly I forgot life's kindness just to focus on this single, tiny misfortune and pain. Same way I focused on a person's loud voice or slowness, and hating him for it, instead of appreciating—loving—the totality of his being.

I was frightened and impressed by how selfish these bodies made us.

On the day I fell, Dumangan returned to his true form and removed my scrapes with a wave of his hand.

And I began to wonder: Why can't we do the same?

And this question led to more questions, and these questions led to a new longing.

Regina, on the day your mother decided to stop visiting Luciano, we were standing in the trees outside the perimeter of the Maximillian Fortes Center. We saw children in groups of threes or fives being led from one building to another. The children walked slowly, uncertainly, as if they were blindfolded.

"I once looked through one of the windows and saw a child being covered with a white sheet," one of us said, but in truth, we weren't concerned about the children. We were blind to them. We were blind to everything that was in front of us.

"Perhaps we could ask him," one of us said, referring, of course, to Dumangan.

"Ask him to lend us his power?"

"Just a little bit. Just for a little time."

"Can a god's power even be transferred?"

"Why not?"

"It is not a bushel of fruit that can just change hands."

"We do not know that."

"There are a lot of things that we do not know."

"We do not know how it feels," one of us said. "Don't you want to know how it feels? To be invincible? Even for just a little while?"

"*Just* a little while?"

"More?"

"If he could give us bodies, if he could make us finite, then he should be able to make us invincible forever."

And a chill ran through us, because these words felt dangerous.

"It is not like we would hurt him."

We laughed in relief.

"No. No, of course not. How ridiculous."

"Although we easily could. While in mortal form, he is our equal."

"That's true."

Pause.

"But perhaps we could just ask him, and he would say yes."

"What is this?"

We heard the violent rustling of leaves, the crisp sound of wood breaking as branches were shoved aside to make a path. I glanced over my shoulder and saw a beautiful woman making her way to us, her black dress flowing like water to the ground. I couldn't stop staring at her. For a second her eyes turned red, and the surface of her dress vibrated as if it were made not of cloth, but of birds.

She smelled like a vast field burning.

"Dumangan's little companions having a conclave?" Hukluban said. She stepped between us and turned, her back to the Center, and looked at us, one by one. We did not want to disrespect her, so we lowered our gaze and tried our very best not to shrink away. She leaned toward me and waved her hand in front of my nose. I saw something sparkle, and realized she was now holding a glass marble between her thumb and forefinger.

She straightened up, and we watched as the clear glass became cloudy, became as dark as coal.

"You are planning something," Hukluban said, smiling at me in wonder, and I felt cold sweat break on my brow. "What could you possibly be planning, little spirit?"

We felt a shadow hovering behind us, and Hukluban's smile widened. She lowered her hand.

"Greetings, Dumangan."

"Hukluban," Dumangan said, and raised an eyebrow. "You are not bothering them, are you?"

"Of course not, Dumangan," she said.

"What have you got in your hand, then?"

She showed her empty palms to him. "Nothing," she said. "Nothing at all."

"We should go," Dumangan said to us, and we started walking away at once, the smell of ashes burning our noses. To the goddess he said, "What are you doing here anyway?"

Hukluban turned her back to him to stare at the Center.

"What I usually do," Hukluban said. "Waiting." She waved goodbye to him, and transformed into a flock of black birds that flew over the Center and beyond.

Dumangan took us to a shallow lake he had found in the woods, but shortly after taking a dip, I broke away from the group to walk deeper into the trees. The Goddess of Death, in the form of a large black dog, walked with me for a silent minute or two before returning to her human form. I knew the woman body she presented was not her true form, because I glanced at her face and I was still alive. No one could witness a god's true form and survive without grave injury. Still, I kept my gaze averted.

"You want to ask me a question," she said.

I kept my eyes focused on my feet.

"Go on, then, little spirit," she said.

I took a deep breath and said, "I knew my Lady could change her form, but I didn't know my Lady could also change thoughts into tangible objects."

"That's not a question, is it?"

I tried again. "Can other gods do the same?"

"No," she said. "I have seen Dumangan transmute a small portion of his power and give it to a sick, bedridden boy, but that was so long ago. Dumangan has a soft heart." She shrugged.

"Gods can share their powers?" I said.

Hukluban fell silent, but her silence was heavy, as though the quiet held an answer.

"You will not hurt yourself now, will you," she said after a moment, walking ahead of me, "little spirit?"

A thirteen-year-old girl came home to her family's house in the Poblacion after spending eight weeks in the Center. The afternoon of her homecoming, she ran out of the kitchen door and through the neighborhood with wide, horrified eyes, like a dog deranged. She was wearing "nice" clothes—meaning a new dress and a pair of shiny leather low-heeled pumps, the kind of clothes and shoes you would wear to church—and she tore her dress and ruined her shoes as she ran through backyards, farms, puddles of water, and a major road, blisters bursting inside her socks, her arms bleeding from hundreds of cuts from wild grass, until she slipped on mud and struck her head on a rock. It was a desolate place, that field where she died. Years later, it would be turned into a road leading to the next town. You could see the road from this window.

We were part of the group that tried to run after her. Tried, because she ran like the wind. She ran like nothing solid could touch her. When her father reached her body—

I remember seeing her father's face, and it was as if he were seeing something so far beyond the realm of reality that he could not accept it. As if this were the last thing he expected to happen. He cried as much out of shock as out of sorrow, as though someone had cut off his limb. I learned later that the girl was enrolled in the Center because—well, I can now say she was manic-depressive, but years ago they described her as "not quite right in the head." They took her home because she wanted to go home, because they thought she was "cured."

I was standing beside Dumangan when the girl finally stopped running. If he could transmute powers to save a mortal life, then the best time to do it would be *now*, wouldn't it?

But he did nothing.

I asked Dumangan why he didn't help the poor girl. When a long time passed without him answering, I asked, "Could you have helped the poor girl?"

He said no. I asked why.

"We don't meddle in mortal affairs," he said. "You know that."

"Then why do they even pray to you?"

"Do they?" He looked amused. "They pray for sun and for rain. They don't pray for my mediation." After a pause he added, "I only meddle when there are other non-mortal hands meddling."

"So otherwise," I said, "mortals are on their own." Left to battle the elements with their frail bodies and left to die should they fall into a deep pit, no matter how hoarse their voices became as they screamed for mercy. But I did not say that.

"Yes," Dumangan said with a smile. "And isn't that beautiful?"

"What else do you want to experience?" one of us asked.

"To fly."

"To swim to the depths and not run out of air."

"To not need air."

"To not need food."

"To live," I said, "forever."

CHAPTER 18

And so, I asked. Each and every one of us wanted to ask Dumangan the same question, but I was the only one who was brave enough to—

But no. Forgive me. I'm not here to blame anyone. I just want to—

Let me continue with this story.

It was harvest season, coinciding with the town fiesta. Dumangan had moved his house to a neighborhood on the roadside, so we were surrounded by boisterous singing, loud laughter. I was at the sink, chopping up vegetables for a stew. Everyone else was—I don't recall now what they were doing. When Dumangan entered the house, everyone else conveniently found an excuse to slip out through the back door. It was just a question, I thought, chopping up a carrot. He could say no. No harm done.

I looked up and realized why the group decided to disperse. Dumangan was with Mapulon, the God of Seasons. He looked like he had just stepped out from one of the neighbors' houses, but he wasn't in true mortal form, like Dumangan. I could feel a force emanating from him. I wondered if anyone else in town felt that, if any of them realized there was a powerful being walking among them.

"Where did everyone else go?" Dumangan asked.

For a moment I couldn't answer.

Dumangan turned to Mapulon, who was staring at me as though he wanted to memorize my face.

"Stop frightening her."

"I wasn't doing anything."

That was when I found my voice. "Greetings, my Lord."

"Greetings," Mapulon said, and stepped closer. "So, you're one of them. What fine work, Dumangan."

"Don't talk about her like that," Dumangan said.

"Like what?"

"Like she's a fixture in this house."

I was not supposed to hear that but I heard it anyway. I turned back to my vegetables, and from a corner of my eye I could see Dumangan looking at me.

"So!" Mapulon said. "I hear today's your last day as a mortal. Three days, is that the agreement?"

I focused on the chopping board.

"I asked you a question," Mapulon said. "Didn't I?"

"It doesn't have to be," I said without looking at him, because I felt a need to punch him in the face. I felt it in my gut like a pain that made my eyes water. I didn't know where this urge came from.

"What's that?" Dumangan said, not unkindly. "Well, speak up now. We're all equals here."

I turned to them and saw Mapulon's face darken at that word. *Equal.*

I began to apologize, but Mapulon cut me off. "No. You tell him what you said."

Dumangan smiled. Go on, then, he seemed to say.

"I said, it doesn't have to be. Our last day, I mean."

Dumangan paused for a moment, then nodded to himself. An almost imperceptible nod. As though he had expected this. Mapulon, on the other hand, looked like was just resisting the urge to slap me. His face screamed, *How dare you? How dare you say this to us?*

"Just three days, little one," Dumangan said. "There is still next year, yes?"

"Her hand is bleeding," Mapulon said.

I looked down and saw a long gash that ran across three of my fingers. Did I hold the knife by its blade? How foolish could I be?

Dumangan moved to touch me. "Here, allow me to—"

Mapulon placed a hand on his chest and turned to me. "Wash the wound with soap and water and press a fresh towel on your hand to staunch the bleeding." I did as I was told. Through the sound of the open tap I heard Mapulon say, "She is mortal. You should allow them to be acquainted with the pains of their bodies."

And beneath all that, the unspoken words: Did you hear what she told you? How dare she?

Before long it was night, and we were nearing the end of our last day. We were having dinner right here in the living room. Dumangan used to have a table here, and that night it groaned with the weight of our food—chicken and pork and fish, rice and vegetables and the hearty stew that I made and bled for—but I couldn't eat.

"What's wrong, little one?" Dumangan asked.

I had been fighting the words for hours, but at that moment I couldn't fight them any longer as they found their way out of my mouth: "We are not equals."

The table fell silent.

"This morning, you said we were equals," I said, "but we were really not."

"Little one—"

"Let me carve a piece of chicken for you," I said, and stood up to grab the knife.

"I understand that you are upset—"

"Not upset," I said, cutting a chunk of meat from the chicken's breast and serving it on his plate. "Just trying to understand the true order of things."

"And what," Dumangan said, "is the true order of things?"

"Some are more important than others," I said. "Some can die without the world grieving them."

"Is that so?"

"Hukluban said you transmuted some of your powers to save a sick boy," I said. "You could have saved that poor girl, but you didn't. And we are alive, aren't we? And yet you won't even let us enjoy this for another day more?"

Dumangan looked at me for a moment and sighed. Somehow this sigh, this dismissive shake of his head, irritated me more than if he had lashed out like Mapulon, more than if he had said, "I will not be spoken to like this."

"Little one," he said. He paused for a beat and looked around the table. "Little ones—is this how you really feel?"

All around the table, the cowards bowed their heads, refusing even to look me or Dumangan in the eye.

Cowards.

To me he said, "This was not a show of might. I gave you this experience so you can learn gratitude."

"Gratitude?" I said. "To whom? To you?"

"To life," he said, "to living," and in my mind's eye I saw a golden field of rice. Rain. A good harvest. I felt ashamed, but acknowledging the shame made me angry, and I'd rather feel angry than feel small.

Don't we all?

To one of us who would later become Doreen I said, "Get up," and she stood up, and I stood behind her and placed the knife across her neck.

"And if I said I would kill her if you didn't relinquish your power to us," I said, "what would you do?"

Everyone, save for Dumangan, pushed back their chairs and stood up, hands hovering in the air, as though I were a bird they were planning to trap.

Dumangan suddenly looked very tired.

"What would you do?" I asked, and pressed the blade against Doreen's neck. I drew blood. Do something, the others said to Dumangan. Please do something.

But he only looked and looked and looked.

"You see now?" I said to them. "You see how little you mean to him?"

And the others looked at him with dimmed eyes, as though they had just finally awakened.

Dumangan sighed, stood up, and walked over to me. "Listen," he said.

I don't recall how it happened, but a second later there was no knife in my hands and there was a blade handle sticking out of Dumangan's chest, as though it had sprouted there. He fell to his knees, his shirt rapidly turning red. He took a deep, ragged breath, and the blood flowing around the wooden handle bubbled. He fell sideways, like a man about to curl for a quick nap, and his breath became rapid and shallow. The look in his eyes—

I would never forget that.

Before he finally died, he must have projected himself across the fields and the houses, because at that very hour his likeness appeared at the foot of the old man Cajucom's bed, making sounds the old man could not understand. Dumangan was choking on his own blood on the floor of his house, so of course he did not make much sense.

I still don't know what he had tried to say to the old man.

Forgive me?

Forgive them?

Maybe not the second one.

I wondered, every night since that night, what he had wanted to say to me.

Listen—

If only I had.

And now—

Now someone else has to tell you the rest of the story.

After that moment, I was—I was indisposed.

I was mourning.

CHAPTER
19

"She was catatonic," Luciano said, and for a moment Regina wondered if he meant the Florina in the story, or herself. She couldn't feel her face. She couldn't feel the floor under her feet.

"This is impossible," she said. "Are you even my brother?"

Luciano looked hurt. "Of course, I'm your brother."

Regina began to cry.

Luciano turned to Doreen. "This isn't right, you said. You think *this* is right?"

"Keep talking," Regina said. "Somebody better keep talking and finish this story or I swear—"

"She was catatonic," Luciano continued, slowly, "for several hours. No one could kill a god and survive with her mind intact. That's what we thought."

Luciano said:

When Dumangan took his last breath, red seeds appeared in his spilt blood. They looked like the bulbs of blossoming tea, only that they were as small as raisins. I took one, and when it bloomed in my hand, I felt a surge of power, painful like a kick to the head, pleasant and intoxicating like wine.

The seeds were his power, transmuted into harvest.

We could no longer see Dumangan then, just the flowers. We divided it equally among ourselves. Florina's portion I placed in a handkerchief. I remember watching the cotton suck up the blood. I folded the corners of the handkerchief over the seeds and placed them in her hands.

She looked at me with her vacant eyes, and the horror came back. Dumangan was dead. We had killed a man—a god—who had trusted us completely, and here we were dividing his power like loot. *What kind of monsters are we?* But even as I asked this I couldn't stop thinking of those red blooms and how *alive* they made me feel.

We swallowed them, one by one, kneeling right there in the pool of his blood, until there was nothing left.

Now energized, we buckled down to the task of moving the body. We moved the house away from the neighborhoods with our newfound power, but we used our arms and hands and legs for the rest of the work. After that was done, we went back inside the house and washed the soil from our skin, cleared the table, and mopped the floor. We emptied the bucket of blood-tinged water several times, but we were working on an—on an *intellectual* level. We were numb. We were not thinking of death; we were thinking, *The floor was dirty and so we had to clean it.*

We could not remove the smell of rust and rot no matter how much we scrubbed and wiped, and so we conjured flowers from thin air, placed them in various places to perfume the room. Soon enough, dusk spirits were clacking on the windows, peering in, wondering how five fellow spirits in mortal bodies managed to produce fragrant sampaguita from nothing.

We looked at each other and thought, Hukluban.

We only then realized our actions would have consequences beyond our guilt and our sorrow.

Hukluban is the Goddess of Death. She doesn't strike mortals to hasten their journey to her. Instead she waits, and she waits patiently.

We fear what we don't understand, and so she is also known as the agent of Sitan, the Ultimate Darkness, even if all she does is stand on the periphery while humans with their free will hack each other to pieces.

We spirits know her as Lady Justice, and her sentence is oblivion.

We were trying to save our sister, you see.

We were trying to save her from oblivion.

We transmuted Florina's memory of that night and turned the red blooms purple with her guilt.

We tied up the handkerchief and buried these flowers of remorse and murder next to Dumangan.

We thought, if Hukluban came to Florina at that instant and asked her what happened, Florina could say, "I don't know," and it would be the truth.

Hukluban appeared inside the house moments later. She wasn't there and then she was, her black dress billowing, the smell of flames burning away the fragrance of our conjured flowers.

"Where is Dumangan?" she asked.

We did not answer.

She stepped forth and we parted, and we did not say anything as she knelt in front of one of us who would become Florina.

"Little spirit," she whispered, and Florina sobbed and covered her eyes, "where is Dumangan?"

Hukluban waved her hand. A glass marble appeared on her palm. She waited. We waited. The marble remained clear.

She stood up without a word, graceful as a rice stalk.

I spoke up before my courage could run away from me, "My Lady, we would like to give you an offering."

She stood with her back to us for a long moment. The silence was deep enough to make me want to take back what I had said.

"An offering for what?" she said, finally, still not facing us.

I suddenly couldn't speak. I was relieved when she spoke, turning to us with a broad sweep of her black dress.

"For my silence?" she said with a small smile. "So, I would turn a blind eye?"

"For your," I said, swallowing hard, sure I would be struck dead right then and there, "mercy."

Florina sobbed behind her.

Hukluban stared at us for what felt like ages.

"What kind of offering?" Hukluban said.

I want to make it clear, Regina, that we didn't kill the children we gave to her.

I want to make it clear that when we found them, they were already dead.

CHAPTER 20

Not wanting to waste time, we moved Dumangan's house to the Center's quadrangle after Hukluban left us. At that hour, we could see just a few lights glowing in the buildings' windows, but several guards were already advancing toward us before the house could even completely materialize.

"Sleep," we said, and the guards fell limp and slept.

We didn't know yet how to do that to everyone at the same time, so some of us had to stay behind to make sure anyone emerging from the building could be stopped.

One of us had to enter the Center.

Doreen said:

I saw Florina the moment I stepped into the grand lobby.

The Florina who truly owned the name.

She was rushing out of a hallway, looking like she had just rolled out of bed, but she was still wearing the short white coat of a doctor in training.

"I saw lights outside," she said, and I said "Sleep," and she fell to her knees and slept.

The room where they took the children was in the basement. The basement was cold, but it wasn't a cold that came from the night air. It was a cold that came from an empty place. There was a guard behind a desk, and I waved my hand to make him sleep in his seat. The door he was guarding was bare, nondescript, made of steel and smoky glass. I waved my hand to open the door and turn on the light inside.

I was greeted by silence. At first glance, it looked like a room filled with children sleeping under thin blankets, their beds placed side by side.

But there was no sound, no one tossing or turning.

No one breathing.

Save for one.

I'm talking about you, Clara.

This is what I've been trying to tell you.

Clara, listen.

Clara, *listen to me.*

Save for Clara, all of the children had pale faces and black lips. Some of them were laid gently, others tossed. They looked grotesque: chins tilted so high they looked like they were on the verge of asking a question; arms or legs twisted at odd angles like the victims of a bombing.

I walked over to her. Clara was in a far corner, on a bed next to the wall.

"Hello," I said.

I could see her shaking under the blanket. After a moment she sat up and leaned against the wall, the blanket pulled up to her chin. Her eyes were bloodshot.

"They're all dead," she said.

I glanced back. The child on the next bed, to my horror, had hair strands caught under her left eyelid. I turned away in an instant.

"You're not," I said.

She looked past me and whimpered, as though she did not want to accept this fact.

"How did they die?" I asked.

She said, "The doctors here make people sick."

"You're not," I said, and she broke down, crying not like a child, but like a soldier in battle, mourning a fresh death.

I felt a change in the air, and I told her to be quiet and hide under the sheet.

Hukluban stood by the door. "Thirty souls," the goddess said when I turned to face her. "Bring the bodies to me."

I counted the beds. There were thirty children, including Clara.

"I will carry you up," I told Clara. "I will carry you up with a pillow and a blanket."

Do not be afraid.

Everyone within the Center was asleep. Curled up on the marble floor, in their seats, on the staircase, on the grass. Hukluban did this. She stood in the quadrangle, in front of the graphite slab.

"Little spirit," she said, "where did you get your power?"

I said nothing.

"You will bring up the bodies with your bare hands," she said.

And that was what we did. It took ages. Eight or more trips up and down those basement stairs and out onto the bare grass, the dead children in our arms. We pulled and shoved them and placed them in position, arranging them around the Goddess of Death in concentric circles. When I carried Clara I whispered to her, "Do not move," and she didn't, and I placed her on the outermost circle, arranged the pillows on top of her so the blanket would retain a shape when the time was right for her to run and leave.

Most of the children were wrapped in their own blankets, so she didn't look out of place. We used the blankets to cover them because we couldn't bear to look at their faces.

When it was time to carry the last four children, one of us said, "We couldn't live in these bodies anymore. These bodies were Dumangan's gifts."

"What do you suggest?" one of us said, and the first one pointed at the children at our feet. We were in the lobby. Outside, Hukluban stood waiting.

"No," I said.

"We have to."

"It is vulgar," I said.

"We will honor their lives," one of us said. "We will honor their lives by living."

We took their *potential,* which was the only thing left to mourn—and harvest—after their lives were snuffed too early. What was left of their lives was round like guavas and tasted just as sweet, and the children's names were Loretta, Luciano, Emil, and Doreen.

Now in children's bodies, it took three of us to drag one of our old bodies out of the building and into the quadrangle. Hukluban said nothing as we did this. If she were surprised or shocked or disgusted by our transformation, we had no way of knowing—her eyes betrayed no emotion.

When all was done, we faced her and said, "It is done."

She said, "Where did you get this power?"

We said nothing.

She said, "Where is Dumangan?"

We said nothing.

She said, "Would you trick the Goddess of Death to get what you want?"

I nearly cried, but we said nothing.

"Do you think you can trick me?" she said, looking at me. "Do you think I forcefully take those who do not wish to come home to me?"

The others turned to me, confused. I thought of Clara, hiding under a blanket, surrounded by the dead. I said nothing.

"I am patient," Hukluban said to us. "One day you will tell me."

I don't know when Clara left, but she left, leaving pillows under the blanket. "May life be kind to you," Hukluban said, and disappeared with the bodies we laid at her feet.

And so.

And so, we walked back to Dumangan's house. I sat next to our fellow spirit and said, "From now on you will be known as Florina." I said, "And you will live in this body until the day we die."

And it was so, because in that brief moment we were gods, and whatever we said came to life.

And I said, "From now on this place will remain hidden from anyone without my invitation."

And we said, "From now on the Center and everyone and everything that dwelled within will be erased from everyone's memory."

And it was so.

Florina said:

I crawled away from the corner where I had fallen and examined the house with new eyes. Eventually I left through the kitchen door, to the earth where they buried him, and found the flowers buried there. I ate every single bloom, driven by something more than memory, and details of my deed returned to me, one by one, and they reside within me still.

They thought I have forgotten but I have not. All these years, I have remembered. Every single day I sat here in this house alone and did nothing but remember.

Emil said:

Our power was finite.

Doreen conserved a little of her power and volunteered to take care of Florina.

But that was it. Before morning came, we were mortal again.

Hungry, thirsty, and tired, we walked out of the quadrangle and fell asleep. We were found hours later by a Cajucom farmhand, who took some of us back to our homes, and some of us to the police station to track down our families outside Heridos.

The families seemed glad enough to see us back.

Florina said:

Imagine for a moment that you are your own mother, Regina. You are thirty-three years old, married to a thirty-four-year-old. You have a seven-year-old son who has just turned eight. When he was seven, he disappeared but was returned to you a short while later—or, at least, it was a short while in your mind. Sometimes, though, in your dreams, you see him in a building you've never seen before, and he is hitting your thigh, and he is accusing you of abandonment.

He behaves differently now. He is quiet. Sometimes you catch him staring at you. Most days he feels like a stranger.

Two years later you find out you are pregnant, once again, and you give birth to a baby girl, which delights your husband. Your second child tires you the way most children tire their mothers, but she comes home with good grades, with commendations from teachers, with friends. Your older son dotes on her, and you forget that you have dreamt of abandoning him, once upon a time.

When the *hilot* places your daughter on your chest, the name "Florina" comes to you, unbidden. Where did that come from, you wonder, at the same time thinking, What a beautiful name. But the name bites back; someone else owns it. And so, you name your daughter something else.

You name her Regina.

PART IV

Wounded Little Gods

CHAPTER 21

Regina felt a hand on her shoulder. She swatted it away, and in an eye blink she was up and delivering a slap to her brother's face, the force of it making her palm sting. Clara cried softly somewhere in the dark kitchen. Everyone seemed to be in tears, and Regina was annoyed to feel the wetness on her cheeks. She felt Florina brush up against her back. She turned to her, and Florina said, "I have not been out of this house for a long, long time."

She burst out of the door before anyone could react. Wait, Regina thought, failing to turn the thought into sound as she herself ran out of the house and stretched a hand toward Florina. Florina grasped her hand firmly in hers, and the two ran across grass and mud and sand, places that looked alien to Regina, or did the darkness just distort the land and render it unfamiliar? The others followed in pursuit. She could dimly hear Luciano calling her in the distance.

Regina! Regina!

Regina, come back!

How long did they run? Some miles back she had lost her shoes, and now she ran barefoot, her soles raw and bleeding. Regina felt grass brushing against her ankles and Florina fell to her knees, bringing her down with her.

Regina looked around and realized they were on the Cajucom property, just outside the Center.

(What Center?)

There was a black dog in front of them. An enormous black dog, a dog as big as a house. Regina was afraid.

"Regina!" Luciano sounded closer now. "Regina, let go of her hand!"

The dog was now a woman, wrapping a black shawl around her body.

Florina was crying hard. Regina could hardly understand what she was saying, but she heard *Forgive me and I was wrong* and *I am so tired, Mother.*

"I told you I was patient," the woman said. "I knew you would tell the story, sooner or later."

There were more shapes behind her. Children, Regina thought, the realization like a punch to her stomach.

"Everyone does," the woman said.

The children pressed closer. They were just outlines, shadows; Regina couldn't see their faces.

"Come sleep with me, little spirit," the woman said, reaching out to Florina.

"Thank you for mercy," Florina whispered.

"Regina!" Luciano screamed, more urgent now. "Regina, *let go of her hand!*"

"Let go of her hand, daughter," someone said. Someone untangled her fingers from Florina's cold hand, and another gripped her shoulders and pressed her close, blocking her view of the woman in black. Regina smelled ylang-ylang in the air. The man embracing her smelled like rain.

"Hukluban will show her true form," the man said. "She can blind you."

I am not your daughter, Regina wanted to say, but a brightness came from behind him, so intense it was almost tangible, and Regina closed her eyes.

Luciano ran faster when Hukluban appeared and he saw that Florina and Regina were still holding hands. *Regina! Let go of her hand!* he shouted at the top of his lungs, once, twice, his voice becoming hoarse, his throat getting sore, trying to get through to her, through the dream-haze where she resided now. *Stop!* someone said, and suddenly Em was beside him, his hand on his nape, pushing his head down.

A brightness as dazzling as life.

"I have to admit," a familiar voice said, "that I am not as patient as Hukluban."

Luciano lay on his side, crying. "My sister," he said to the God of Seasons, who was bending over him like a doctor. "Please."

"You and I both know that she is not your sister."

"Is my sister safe?"

Mapulon just stared at him. Amihan stood behind him, her hand on his shoulder.

"Yes," she said to Luciano, her voice a gentle breeze on his cheek.

Gratitude and relief washed over him, and Luciano was racked with sobs once again. "Oh, thank you," he said. "Thank you, thank you."

"Where did you bury Dumangan?" Mapulon said, voice as hard as steel.

"Here," Loretta said, when Luciano failed to answer. "We buried him here." She burst into tears. "I'm so *sorry.*"

"Clara," Amihan said. "Take my hand, child. I will return you to your family."

Clara stood up, fell, stood up. When she fell again, Doreen placed her arms around her waist, whispering to her through her tears, but Clara shook her off with a violent jerk and took Amihan's hand.

Doreen knelt next to Luciano. "What will happen to us now?"

"You revealed this to Regina," Mapulon said. "It seems that you *want* to be caught. Why?"

"I wanted to make amends," Doreen said. She wiped her tears, but fresh tears came, and her cheeks were wet again in a matter of seconds.

"I admire your courage to act on this," Mapulon said, "which certainly can't be said of your friends here. And yet how cowardly of you to resort to games, to drop bread crumbs when you could have just approached Regina and Clara, and told them the truth." He stood up. "Told *us* the truth."

"I didn't know how," Doreen said.

"You wanted to make amends, you said."

"I wanted to make things *right*." Doreen cried. "Florina is dead—"

"She was never truly alive, child."

"—and now you can take my life if you wish."

"Your life?" he said. "And tell me, what will that achieve?"

Doreen looked frustrated. "It will be my punishment!" she said. "It will make things *right!*"

"Can you bring Dumangan back?"

Doreen looked confused. "I—"

"No," Mapulon said. "You can't."

Doreen's eyes turned glassy with tears. "I can't," she said in a small voice.

"Then do not presume," Mapulon said, "that you can ever make things right."

Doreen covered her face.

"But what will happen to us now?" Loretta asked, wringing the hem of her shirt.

No one answered her. Amihan and Mapulon, with Clara in tow, left them without another word, and the wounded little spirits stood up, glanced at each other with fear and sadness, as if they were standing together on the gallows. Luciano remained on his knees, his tears falling, and Em squeezed his shoulders to help him stand up.

Luciano shook his head.

"I'll see you in the morning," Em said, but even to his ears his words sounded like a lie. He and Doreen and Loretta turned away from each other and took their own solitary paths out of the farm.

It was dark when Regina opened her eyes again. A man and a woman were standing in the field behind the barbed wire of the Cajucom farm. CAJUCOM PROPERTY PRIVATE PROPERTY NO TRESPASSING the sign said. For some reason, she could see rice stalks on what she remembered as a barren plot of land, the *palay* golden and heavy. Regina moved closer. She found a gap in the fence and passed through, gently parting the *palay*. There was a man and a woman standing there. The man was wearing a suit and the woman was in a beautiful white dress, looking as if they're dressed for a—

No, not a wedding.

A funeral.

They knelt on the ground. Another man, in jeans and a plain shirt, lay on the ground between them. Blood pooled from a wound on his chest. The woman stood up and tied her hair with a black ribbon, the ribbon unfurling in the soft breeze. She picked up a shovel and dug a hole in the ground. Her companion brushed back the dead man's hair, and cleaned the blood with a handkerchief. After a moment the task proved to be too much for him and he began to cry. He wiped his tears with the bloodied rag.

The grave was ready. Together the man and the woman in funeral clothes lowered the body into the soil. The man waved his hand, conjuring flowers from thin air—stargazer lilies, alstroemeria, gerberas—flowers vibrant in pink, lavender, and dark purple, the color of a fading day. He placed the flowers on the body's chest. Farewell, he said. Farewell, the woman said. The body said nothing.

The woman shoveled soil into the hole until the body was completely buried. The man and the woman reached out for each other. The woman placed an arm around the man's waist, supporting him and leading him through the *palay*. The woman sang as they walked, her voice carrying across the field like the wind that now shook the rice stalks and sent a chill up Regina's spine.

A tree would grow on that farm, a strange tree that no one had ever seen before. It would bear no fruit, but its blossoms would be as red as blood in the early morning, before fading to white and transparent nothingness at dusk. Its fragrance, also dependent on a day's progress, would fade as well, from pungent sweetness to memory.

CHAPTER 22

A blink, and Regina was back in her room, in her house. There were no wounds on her feet. Her clothes and skin were spotless. It was as if the past few hours (days? years?) did not happen.

"Aren't you going to have dinner?" her mother called up from downstairs.

But they happened. She remembered.

She walked down the stairs, and at the first landing stood behind the banister watching her mother and father set the table. Parents are like gods to their children, Regina thought. Their word is the law and their rule is absolute. But they are fallible, just like anyone else. They have dreams and wants, just like anyone else.

And what do parents want in a child?

They want a child who can love them back.

Years ago, her parents had a child who was stubborn and violent, and they turned this child away because they couldn't love him without the merest promise of that love's reciprocation. But who could? Could she blame them? Who was strong enough to continue loving even when that love was not returned?

Regina watched her parents set the table and understood with certainty that no one's love was truly unconditional.

Someone was knocking on the door. Regina walked down the stairs.

"There you are," her father said, and she thought, *Here I am.* She opened the door and stared at the gate, at the small pool of moonlight on the road outside. A breeze blew. There was no one there.

CHAPTER 23

The next day, she woke up early to pack up her things for her commute back to Quezon City. Before she left, she spooned a small serving of Pancit Malabon into a lidded container. She left the kitchen a mess. Instead of getting on the Cubao-bound bus, she took a jeep and got off at Paombong, and walked down the path with the suffocating bougainvillea bushes. Dorothea Fortes, MD, General Practitioner, had just seen a patient but she's free now, her secretary announced. Regina entered the clinic and saw the doctor smoking a cigarette, facing her window and her garden beyond it. Dr. Fortes seemed delighted to see her, accepting the lidded container with both hands.

"Pancit Malabon!" she said. "My favorite! I will have this for lunch. Sit down, dear."

She indicated a small stool behind the desk. Regina took it and sat down beside her.

"I just wanted to thank you for seeing my friend," she said. "And, how is she?"

Regina had not seen Clara since— "Better," she said.

"Good."

"I have a question."

Dr. Fortes blinked at the smoke wafting in her face and took a drag on her cigarette. "Yes?"

"These subpar children," Regina said, wincing at the word, "that you mentioned before: have you ever considered that maybe all they need is compassion and guidance? Maybe, with some help, they will grow up to become, I don't know—artists?" She felt like a drowning person trying desperately to keep her head above the water. "Doctors?"

Dr. Fortes scoffed, and Regina felt weary, and defeated. *"Please,"* the doctor said. "I highly doubt that."

The doctor took a drag, directed the smoke at her ceiling. Sunlight bounced off the bright green leaves of her garden.

"Beautiful day, isn't it?" she said.

"Yes," said Regina, looking at the flowers. She felt like crying. "It is."

Back in the city. The lady's dorm where she rented space was near the university campus, so it was packed with undergrads and board examinees. The faces changed but the worries and annoyances remained the same: papers, reviews, thesis, advisor consultations, rusty water from the shower, missing block of cheese from the shared fridge, and "Reg, what are you doing sitting there?"

This question from a freshman, a new girl in the dorm. Regina tried to remember her name and couldn't. Regina was sitting on the ground behind the gate, still surrounded by her bags and leftovers of a take-out lunch she couldn't finish. The freshman who was sorting through readings in the outdoor sala asked if Regina got locked out of her room.

"I'm okay," Regina said without looking up. "I'm just resting."

Regina resolved to get back to her feet once the freshman went back to whatever she was doing, but she felt so tired.

Someone knocked on the gate a half hour later. Regina hoped the freshman would see who it was, but the girl was busy stapling papers. Regina sighed, got up, and opened the gate.

Luciano was standing there, every inch of him carrying last night's trauma that had somehow been erased from her own body. Cuts on his face, deep gashes in his arms. Feet covered in ointment and bandage strips. Eyes brimming with tears. Regina could see his car parked nearby. Not running, not idling. Parked and locked. A hope, a wish.

"Who is it?" the freshman asked.

Luciano pleaded with his eyes.

She never really knew her brother, poor Luciano that no one understood, that no one wanted. What she knew was this spirit, who had been with her through all the years of her life. Him whom she loved and who loved her.

"It's just my brother," she said, and stepped back to let him in.

Author's Notes

This is a work of fiction, but aspects of the story are based on certain historical facts. Please note though that I have reshaped these facts to fit the narrative, and so I implore interested readers to check out resource materials or consult with experts to see the full picture.

The unnamed "American director...[who] infected Bilibid inmates with cholera" is based on Richard Pearson Strong. According to "Richard Pearson Strong and the iatrogenic plague disaster in Bilibid Prison, Manila, 1906" by E. Chernin of the Department of Tropical Public Health, Harvard School of Public Health, Boston, Massachusetts, "In November 1906, Richard Pearson Strong, then head of the Philippine Biological Laboratory, inoculated 24 men—inmates of Manila's Bilibid Prison—with a cholera vaccine that somehow had been contaminated with plague organisms; 13 men died." Strong was found negligent of locking up his incubators and "for leaving a visiting physician alone in the laboratory, where he might have mixed up the cholera and plague cultures on the fateful day." The Attorney General later found Strong innocent of criminal negligence. Strong was said to be "despondent" over what happened in Bilibid.

The phrase "civilized and uncivilized" came from Dr. Strong's obituary published in the British Medical Journal on November 13, 1948.

I first heard of the Tondo Conspiracy from my history lessons but I have to admit I know little about it save for the surface details. "Esteban Taes" appears as "Esteban Tasi" and "Estevan Taes" in some texts; I decided to use the first spelling.

I have read about eugenics for years and cannot point to a definitive resource material, but I remember reading "Forced sterilization nurse: 'I can see now that it was so wrong'" (March 24, 2014) by Lori Jane Gliha of Aljazeera America and being struck by it. As always, I coped with my horror and dismay by writing a story.

Other reading materials that I found informative and helpful before and during the writing of this short novel: "Migration, local development and governance in small towns: two examples from the Philippines" (International Institute for Environment and Development, 2009) by Charito Basa and Lorna Villamil with Violeta de Guzman; and Andrew Solomon's gorgeously written and eye-opening "Far from the Tree: Parents, Children and the Search for Identity" (Scribner, 2012).

Special thanks to Paul Xymon Garcia for confirming the translation of "Estaba herido de muerte." Special thanks as well to Paolo Chikiamco for publishing "Philippine Pantheons" on Rocket Kapre.

My deepest gratitude as always to Nida Ramirez, Kyra Ballesteros, and the rest of the Visprint team; Jaykie and the Lazarte family; and my own family for the love and support.

— *Eliza Victoria*
2015, Makati, Philippines

About the Author

ELIZA VICTORIA is the author of several books including the Philippine National Book Award-winning *Dwellers* (2014), this novel, *Wounded Little Gods* (2016), the graphic novel *After Lambana* (2016, a collaboration with Mervin Malonzo), and the science fiction novel-in-stories, *Nightfall* (2018). Her fiction and poetry have appeared in several online and print publications, most recently in *LOTAR: The Journal of Southeast Asian Speculative Fiction, The Dark Magazine, Dark Regions Press's Stranded: Lone Survivor Deserted Island Horror Stories*, and *The Apex Book of World SF* Volume 5. Her work has won prizes in the Philippines' top literary awards, including the Carlos Palanca Memorial Awards for Literature. Her one-act plays (written in Filipino) have been staged at the Virgin Lab-Fest at the Cultural Center of the Philippines. For more information, please visit http://elizavictoria.com.

Also by Eliza Victoria: